用簡單英語和老外聊不停

好流利！
我的第一本
英語會話與文法

附 MP3

施孝昌◎著

哈福

用簡單英語和老外聊不停

「學英語好難噢！單字記了又忘，文法規則那麼多，詞類又有變化……；我的英語不好，講錯了很難為情的……。」

類似這種不愉快的「共同體驗」，是眾多學英語的人都有的。

Are you one of them?——你也跟他們一樣，有這種挫折感嗎？

If yes,——如果是的話，讓作者告訴你真正問題所在，你會發現，說一口流利的英語其實很簡單，有中學英語程度就夠了。

單字記了又忘，確實是很頭疼的事，像作者剛剛問你的：

「你也跟他們一樣，有這種挫折感嗎？」

我來舉個例子，下班或放學之前，你向同事、同學宣告可以回家了，你想說：

「我今天的工作全都搞定了。」

「搞定」怎麼說？搞定就是「做完」嘛。那「做完」又該怎麼說？

I am done for the day.

六個英文單字，其中最長的done也不過四個字母。I am done就是「我做完了。」、「我做好了。」、「我都搞定了。」，這句話根本用不上像finished這樣的字眼的。

就如I am done.是「我做完了」，任何場合你都這麼說，自然、清晰、流利，這就是學英語的重點。

「我從小就開始學英語，為什麼到現在還不能跟老外聊天？」

「學英語會話，到底要學多少年，才能流利順口、應用自如呢？」

我經常被問到這樣的問題。

沒看過我的書的人，通常會被我的回答嚇一跳，因為我的答案是，英語會話是現學現會！不用良辰吉日，不需一年、兩年、十年，就是現學現會，這麼簡單！

把英語會話學好，不是「不可能的任務」。

記住我的名言 ：英語很簡單，因為美國白癡也會說英語！聰明的我們，能力會不如一個白癡嗎？所以，英語會話是絕對可以學好的。

這本書的目的，就是要幫你徹底提高英語會話能力，讓你建立自信，發現學英語會話，原來這麼有意思。

讀了這本書，你會發現英語會話突然變得很簡單，那是因為你的英語會話能力已經徹底精進了！

不論你的性別、年齡、職業、興趣是什麼，只要你的動機，是在最短的時間內，徹底增進你的英語會話能力，這本書就是為您而寫，最適合您學習。具體的方法在書中的每一單元都已有詳盡說明，你過去學英語的情形，都不用再提，這是一個新的開始，你就按著每個單元，一步一步地增強你的英語會話能力吧。

純正英語的用字是很簡單的，大可不必為了單字難背而煩惱，只要有一本解說很詳盡、例句很淺易、應用面很廣泛的教材，你根本不必擔心文法規則、詞類變化。

本書都是學英語的重點、都是最純正的美國英語，你可以學到真正美式思考，美式語言表達法，絕不讓你空背無用的中文式、日文式的洋經濱句子。

就像每一本美國AA Bridgers公司所製作的美語教材一樣，你只要跟著MP3配合老師的示範，每學一句話，立刻就在任何場合加以應用，你會學得很快，很有成就。

本書每單元除了有詳細的解說，讓你徹底理解之外，還三個標準的實際英語會話，讓你學習如何在真正的生活、旅遊、上班、商務、學校、人際關係等場合中，使用最常用的英語會話。你不用死背，只要按解說去徹底瞭解使用的時機、方法。

會話裡有兩種加套色的句子，是最重要的學習重點。一種是短句，表示那是各種場合、天天用得上的純美語，你學了就隨時可以使用，應該取代你平常說的國語、台語或日語，例如：學了That's nice of you.（你人真好。）之後，凡是有人幫你任何忙，你原是說「謝謝」，今後你就說Thank you, that's nice of you.

另一種加套色的句子是特別經過解釋的句子，就是要你徹底理解地方，學了這個句子就可以很貼切地用美語會話表達自己的想法或真正的意思，也就是「詞可達意」的意思。只要在字面上按場合稍做更動，你的美語就很道地、很純正。

本書把最常用字彙和最不花精神，就可以記起來的慣用語都列出來，並且隨後都附有例句。一個字若是因詞類不同而有不同意思，你會看到標有名、動、形等，表示名詞、動詞、形容詞。

【學習最純正美語的方法】

就像所有美國AA Bridgers公司出版的英語學習系列書籍，本書都是純正的美語，沒有洋涇濱。

本書的注音用的是K.K.音標，以美國受過高等教育的人士所說英語發音為注音標準。你可以跟著CD學習，效果更好、發音和語調更準確。

真正的美語用字都很簡單，從本書你一定會發現學好英語會話的訣竅。學了本書之後，你的美語會話能力已經徹底增進了，再針對你個人的需要，專門學習你所需要的範圍內的單字、用詞。很快的，你就是個美語專家了！

CONTENTS

第2篇 必需要理解

要求、義務、徵詢、意願的說法

第3篇 英語會話

假設、願望、猜測、懊悔、喜歡的應用

第4篇　　人、事、時、地、物的特殊用法

第1篇　一定要知道

- 能力
- 命令
- 許可
- 懷疑……的說法

01 I can speak English.
我會說英語。

文法句型解析

❑ 學英語會話，最重要的是把自己已經學過的東西，徹底理解、應用，這樣的學法最快，學起來也最不會忘。而英語會話應用最多，但我們最不會的，就是用英語表達自己的能力、看法和意見，相信很多人一定以為那很難，所以每回想到英語會話，就只能停止在How are you? Fine, thank you. 的階段，無法再增進了。我要教你的就是用你必定已經學過的東西，讓你徹底理解它的用法，怎樣用，什麼時候用，你只要順著學習，你的英語會話能力，就可獲得徹底的突破！首先我們從Can這個字來著手。你一定知道can是「能」的意思，但在英語對話中，它又有很多意義上的不同，怎樣用英語才會順口又達意呢？

❑ Can最普通的用法就是在表示「有能力做某事」，你如果說I can do something.我能夠做某事。那就表示，你如果想要做那件事，就沒有任何事情可以阻止你去做。換句話說就是，你能力夠，或是你已學會怎麼做，或是你已得到許可，或者是實際上是可行的。總之你有那個自由去做，不受體力、能力、或其他任何因素的限制。

❑ 所以當你學英語之後，你就會說英語，要用can，說I can speak English.同樣地，你可以說I can swim.我會游泳。I can play tennis.我會打網球。

❑ 某人因為體格很好，所以在體力上有能力做某些事，也是用can，例如：He can lift a kid with one hand.他可以用單手把一個小孩子舉起來。

- 若有人問你「你七點鐘可以到嗎？」，他是在問你「有沒有任何事情會讓你七點鐘不能到」，這個情形，不管是問的或回答的，都是用can，問Can you come at 7:00?你若七點鐘可以到，就說I can come at 7:00.同樣地，在《標準會話二》裡，你說I can wire for more.我可以匯更多的錢來。，表示你可以把錢匯來，不會遇到任何阻礙的。

- 不管為了什麼原因，總之，某件事你就是沒辦法做到，那就用can的否定can't，例如：你要出去，需要找個保姆(baby-sitter)幫忙看小孩，但就是找不到，英語的說法就是I can't find a baby-sitter.同樣地，若有人邀請你參加宴會，但因為某個原因你不能參加，你要告訴對方，I can't come to your party.

標準會話一

A Are you going to make it to the meeting Wednesday night?
你星期三晚上可以來參加會議嗎？

B I want to, but I can't find a baby-sitter.
我想來參加，但我找不到看小孩的保姆。

A My daughter could watch your kids for you, if that will help.
我女兒可以幫你看小孩，如果那樣可以幫得上忙的話。

B Really?
真的嗎？

Great!
太好了。

Can she come at 7:00?
她可以七點來嗎？

A No problem.
沒有問題。

I'll bring her by then.
我就那個時候把她帶過來。

B Thanks!
謝謝你。

You're a lifesaver.
你真是一位救命恩人。

標準會話二

A My car is in the shop again.
我的車又進廠修理了。

B What's wrong with it this time?
這一回它又出了什麼問題了呢？

A Oh, just some engine trouble.
哦，只是一些引擎的問題。

B If you need a lift somewhere, I can drive you.
你要是需要有人載你去什麼地方，那我可以載你去。

A That's nice of you.
你做人真好。

B Call me if you need me.
你要是需要我的話，就請打電話給我。

標準會話三

A Oh no!
唉呀，糟糕！

It's 5:00 and I forgot to go to the bank!
已經五點了，我忘了到銀行去！

B Can't you go tomorrow?
你明天再去不行嗎？

A No, we are leaving on vacation tomorrow and I needed cash.
不行，我們明天就要出發去度假了，但我需要現款。

B Well, I could lend you a hundred dollars, if that would help.
那麼我可以借給你一百塊錢，如果那樣可以幫上忙的話。

A That would see me through until I can wire for more.
那樣可以讓我先救救急，一直到我打電報請銀行給我匯款過來。

Thank you so much!
真是太謝謝你了。

B You're welcome.
不用客氣。

第1篇 一定要知道

❶	**baby-sitter** ['bebɪ͵sɪtɚ] 保姆	We need a baby-sitter to watch the kids. 我們需要一個保姆來看小孩。
❷	**shop** [ʃɑp] 修理廠；修理店	My watch is in the shop getting fixed. 我的錶正在店裡修理。
❸	**engine** ['ɛndʒɪn] 引擎	The engine runs the car. 引擎帶動車輛。
❹	**lifesaver** ['laɪf͵sevɚ] 救命恩人	My friend helps me all of the time. She is a lifesaver. 我的朋友從頭到尾幫我的忙，她是我的救命恩人。
❺	**wire** [waɪr] 打電報	She wired for money from the bank. 她打電報給銀行要求匯款。

慣用語加強

❶ to make it 辦得到

Did you make it on time to the party?
你準時參加宴會了嗎？

❷ to see（人）through 度過

I have enough clothes to see me through the summer.
我有足夠的衣服，度過這個夏天。

❸ a lift 搭載

I need to go to school. Can you give me a lift?
我需要到學校去，你可以載我去嗎？

02 Can you believe this weather?

這種天氣真難以置信啊!

文法句型解析

❏ Can也可以用在口語中說「Can you believe +某件事?」,對所發生的事「表示不可置信」的說法。例如:一轉眼夏天又來到了,令你不能不慨嘆地說Can you believe it's summer already?已經是夏天了,真難以置信呀?或是前一天晚上的籃球賽打得出乎意料之外,隔天見面的第一句話,當然是Can you believe that basketball game last night?

標準會話一

A **Can you believe it's summer already?**
已經是夏天了,真難以置信呀!

B **This year is really flying by!**
今年過得真是飛快。

A **Yes, it seems just yesterday we were starting the semester.**
是呀,這學期開學才好像是昨天的事情。

Now it's almost time for finals.
現在都已經快到期末考了。

D **Let's study together tonight at my house.**
我們今天晚上就在我家一起念書吧!

A Can you believe how much our rent has gone up?
我們的房租提到那麼高，真是難以相信！

B I know!
我曉得！

Ninety dollars is a lot!
九十美元是太多了！

A Why do you think the landlords raised the rent so high?
你認為房東為什麼要把房租提高那麼多呢？

B They have done a lot of renovations.
他們做了很多新的整修。

A Yes, but ninety dollars is too much.
那倒是，不過九十美元還是太多了。

A Can you believe that basketball game last night?
昨天晚上的籃球賽，真是令人難以置信！

B Why?
怎麼會？

What happened?
出了什麼事嗎？

A Oh, you didn't watch it?
啊，你沒有看啊？

B No, I missed it.
沒有，我錯過了。

A My team won the game in the last five seconds!
我那一隊到最後五秒鐘才贏得比賽！

B Wow!
哇！

I wish I had watched it!
我希望我昨天晚上有看！

增加字彙能力

❶	**already** [ɔl'rɛdɪ] 已經	I already did my homework. 我已經把我的作業做了。
❷	**semester** [sɪ'mɛstɚ] 學期	The semester starts on September first. 這學期是九月一日開學。
❸	**renovations** [ˌrɛnə'veʃənz] 整修	I am doing some renovations on my house. 我把我的房子做了一番整修。

④	**team** [tim] 團隊	I cheered for my team. 我為我的那一隊加油打氣。
⑤	**wish** [wɪʃ] 希望	I wish I had been with you. 我真希望我當時跟你在一起。

❶ flying by 過得很快

My day is flying by.
我的日子過得真快。

❷ gone up 高漲

Gas prices have really gone up.
汽油價格真是高漲呀。

SCHOOL

03 Can I carry the bag?

我可以幫你提行李嗎？

文法句型解析

❏ Can可以用來表示你想提供幫忙，或提供某些東西，這種用法都是說「Can I+你想幫忙的事情或你想提供的東西？」，例如：你看到一個人提著行李，你願意幫忙提(carry the bag)，你就可以趨前去問Can I carry the bag?或是有客人來，你想倒杯咖啡給他(get him a cup of coffee)，你可以這麼問，Can I get you a cup of coffee?

❏ 想提供幫忙，或提供某些東西也可以用「I can +你想幫忙的事情或你想提供的東西。」例如：你的朋友有事外出，卻找不到保姆看小孩，你願意幫她看小孩(watch the kid)，你就可以告訴她，I can watch the kid for you.或是你的朋友車子壞了，你願意載他，同樣用can，I can drive you.這個用法，在第一單元的標準會話裡也運用上了，你可以回去看看，順便比較、溫習can的另一種用法。

❏ 當然你也可以說Can I buy you a drink?用在想請對方喝一杯時。

❏ 注意：can表示「提供幫忙或提供某樣東西」時，也可以用could，只是語氣上比較客氣。總之，你用can或could都可以的。所以你也可以說Could I carry the bag?或I could watch the kid for you.

標準會話一 在餐廳裡，A：侍者，B：顧客

A Are you finished with your meal, Sir?
先生，你用餐完畢了嗎？

B Yes, thank you.
是的，謝謝你。

A Can I get you anything else?
你還需要我幫你拿什麼東西嗎？

B Just the check, please.
請把帳單送過來就好。

標準會話二 在飯店，A：服務生，B：旅客

A Can I help you with your bag, Miss?
小姐，我可以幫忙提行李嗎？

B Yes, thank you.
可以，謝謝你。

It is quite heavy.
行李很重哦。

A Your room number, please?
你的房間號碼是幾號？

B I'm in Room 617.
我是617號房。

A Very good.
很好。

I'll take the bag there.
我會把行李提到那兒。

標準會話三

A Wow, you sure bought a lot of stuff at the store.
哇，你從店裡買了好多東西哦。

B They had a great sale!
他們在大拍賣呢？

A Can I give you a hand with some of those boxes?
我可以幫你拿這些盒子嗎？

B Sure.
當然。

Let's bring them into the kitchen.
那我們把它們帶到廚房吧。

增加字彙能力

①	**sale** [sel] 大拍賣	He went to the sale at the store. 他到店裡的大拍賣去買東西了。

②	**meal** [mil] 餐食	The waitress served my meal. 女侍者幫我服務餐食。
③	**heavy** [ˈhɛvɪ] 重	The heavy bag was hard to carry. 重行李很難提。
④	**bought** [bɔt] 買 （buy的過去式）	They bought a new car. 他們買了一輛新車。
⑤	**kitchen** [ˈkɪtʃən] 廚房	I fixed dinner in the kitchen. 我在廚房做晚飯。
⑥	**stuff** [stʌf] 物品	What's the stuff in your bag? 你袋子裡是什麼東西呀？

慣用語加強

❶ to give a hand with 幫忙

Give me a hand with the door, please.
請幫我開開門。

❷ room number 房間號碼

The hotel clerk gave us our room number.
旅館服務員把房間號碼給我們。

04 You can clean the room first.

你可以先清理房間。

文法句型解析

❏ **Can**也可以用來「給予指示或要求」，例如：你的秘書問你有什麼事要他做，你可以指示他說「先打這封信」，說法就是 You can start by typing this letter.又如你有客人要來，你開始指揮全家人做事時說，Mary can do the shopping, **and I'll do the cooking.** John can do the washing-up.瑪莉去買菜，我來做飯。約翰可以做清理工作。

標準會話一

A I'm done with my assignment.
我所有指定的工作都做完了。

What else should I do?
你還有什麼別的要我做嗎？

B You can start by typing this letter.
你可以開始打這一封信。

The boss needs it.
老闆需要這封信。

A Do you have some company letterhead?
你有沒有公司正式信紙？

B Yes.
有的。

It's in the top drawer of the desk.
信紙就在桌子最上層的抽屜裡。

A Okay, I'll get right on it.
好的，我馬上就開始做。

標準會話二

A What do you need me to do today, Ms. Wang?
王小姐，你今天需要我做什麼事嗎？

B You can start by vacuuming the living room.
你可以先從客廳吸塵開始。

Then you can mop the kitchen floor.
然後你就把廚房的地板抹一抹。

A Do you need me to clean the bathroom?
妳需要我清理浴室嗎？

B Yes, and please fold the laundry, too.
好的，也請你把衣服摺一下。

標準會話三

A I'm here to work on the proposal.
我是來做企劃案的。

B Welcome to the team.
歡迎加入本團隊。

You can begin by organizing these files.
你可以把這些檔案整理一下。

A Do you want them in alphabetical order?
你要這些檔案按照英文字母的順序排列嗎？

B Of course.
當然。

Then put them in the file cabinet.
整理完請擺在檔案櫃裡。

增加字彙能力

❶	**assignment** [ə'saɪnmənt] 指定工作	Do you have any assignments for me to do? 你要給我什麼指定工作做嗎？
❷	**letterhead** ['lɛtɚ'hɛd] 正式信紙	I used letterhead for the official correspondence. 正式書信往來我都用正式信紙。

❸	**drawer** [ˈdrɔɚ] 抽屜	I like this desk; it has many drawers. 我喜歡這張桌子，它有很多抽屜。
❹	**vacuum** [ˈvækjum] 吸塵	We vacuum the carpets once a week to keep them clean. 我們一個禮拜把地毯吸塵一次，以保持清潔。
❺	**proposal** [prəˈpozəl] 企畫案	We hope the client accepts the proposal. 我希望客戶會接受這企畫案。
❻	**cabinet** [ˈkæbənɛt] 櫥櫃	All the files go in the brown metal cabinet. 所有的檔案都歸在咖啡色的金屬櫃裡。
❼	**laundry** [ˈlɔndrɪ] 換洗衣物	My mother always does the laundry in the morning. 我媽媽都是在早上洗衣服。

慣用語加強

❶ get right on it 馬上做

He started his assignment right away; he got right on it.

他即刻開始做他的指定工作，他算是馬上做了。

❷ in alphabetical order 按照字母順序

I put the list of names in alphabetical order.

我把名單按照字母順序排列。

MP3-6

05 May I go home a little early tonight?
我今晚可以提早回家嗎？

文法句型解析

❏ 表示請求，一般的說法是，用may或can都可以，但是英、美受過教育的人士，尤其是講究英語說法的人，會堅持要用may，既然如此，我們也不必費心神去學那麼多種，表示請求，就用may好了。但是要注意，美國人尤其是年輕人常會用can表示請求，所以當你聽到時，也該知道對方在說什麼。

❏ 這個用法的句型就是「May I+你請求要做的事？」，例如：你想要在星期五請假(have Friday off)，問法就是May I have Friday off?

標準會話一

A May I have an extension on my paper, Professor?
教授，我的報告可以延期交嗎？

B Why do you need an extension?
你為什麼需要延期呢？

A A new report has just been published that will come in handy for my paper.
有一篇新的報告剛剛發表，對我這篇報告很有幫助。

B All right.
好吧。

You may turn your paper in a week later.
你可以延一個禮拜交你的報告。

標準會話二

A May I have Friday off?
我星期五可以請假嗎？

B What for?
為什麼要請假？

A I would like to take a personal day.
我想要請一天事假。

B Do you think you could find a sub?
你認為你可以找到人代班嗎？

A Yes, Mary has already said she can work for me.
可以的，瑪麗已經說她可以代班。

B Then that would be fine.
那就沒有問題。

標準會話三

A May I borrow five dollars from you?
我可以向你借五美元嗎？

B It depends.
那得看情形而定。

What do you need it for?
你為什麼需要這些錢呢？

A I forgot my lunch.
我忘了帶中飯。

I want to go out and get a sandwich.
我要出去買個三明治。

B Take the ten and get me a burger, okay?
拿十塊錢，幫我也買個漢堡好嗎？

A Thanks.
謝謝了。

I'll bring back the change in a jiffy.
我會很快把零錢找給我。

增加字彙能力

❶	**extension** [ɪksˈtɛnʃən] 延期	He missed the deadline but got an extension. 他錯過了截止日期，不過也獲得延期。

❷	**report** [rɪˋport] 報告	I read the newspaper report with great interest. 這篇新聞報導，我是讀得大有興趣
❸	**sub** [sʌb] 替代者 (substitute的簡稱)	Our teacher was sick, so we had a sub. 我們老師病了，所以我們有一位代課老師。
❹	**personal day** [ˋpɝsənḷˋde] 事假	I took a personal day so that I could go see my grandfather. 我請了一天事假，以便探訪我的祖父。
❺	**borrow** [ˋbɑro] 借	She borrowed a cup of milk from her neighbor. 她跟鄰居借了一杯牛奶。

慣用語加強

❶ to come in handy 很有幫助

An extra sweater always comes in handy on a cool day.
在涼爽的天氣裡，有件額外長袖T恤總是很有幫助。

❷ in a jiffy 一瞬間

He came back in a jiffy.
他不一會兒就回來了。

MP3-7

06 I may fly to New York on Tuesday.

我可能星期二搭機到紐約。

文法句型解析

❏ may可以用來表示「某件可能發生的事」，句型是「主詞+may+原形動詞。」例如：你說你可能要請一天假(take one day off)，說法就是I may take one day off.

❏ 你在找瑪莉，但是沒有人知道她在哪裡，但有人跟你說，She may be in her office.她可能在辦公室。或She may be having lunch.她可能在吃午飯。或建議你Ask John. He may know.去問約翰，他可能會知道。大家都是在告訴你一件可能的事情，都用may。

標準會話一 辦公室裡，A：經理，B：秘書

A Please cancel all my afternoon appointments.
請把我今天下午約會都取消。

B Are you going out to lunch?
你要去吃午餐嗎？

A No, because I may need to go see the doctor later.
不，因為我等會可能會去看醫生。

B Are you not feeling well?
你覺得不舒服嗎？

A No. I am having a bad headache.
不舒服，我頭疼得很厲害。

標準會話二

A I may be late tonight, so don't wait up for me.
我今晚上可能晚歸，所以不用一直等我。

B Where are you going?
你要去那裡？

A I have a dinner meeting, remember?
我晚上有個餐會，你忘了嗎？

B Oh, that's right.
噢，對了。

How late will you be?
你會多晚才回來呢？

A I should be home by 11:00, but you never know.
我應該會在十一點以前回來，不過到時候會怎麼樣也不曉得。

標準會話三

A I may change my major.
我也許會改變主修科目。

B Don't you like chemistry?
你不喜歡化學嗎？

A It's interesting, but I think physics is where my interests lie.
化學是很有趣，不過我想我的興趣是在物理。

B You are lucky to have such a good head for science.
你真幸運，有一個那樣好的頭腦學科學。

增加字彙能力

1	**cancel** ['kænsl̩] 取消	She canceled the dentist appointment. 她把看牙醫的掛號取消。
2	**lucky** ['lʌkɪ] 幸運	I was lucky and won the game. 我很幸運贏得比賽。
3	**chemistry** ['kæməstrɪ] 化學	The field of chemistry is always changing. 化學這個領域，一直在改變。

❹	**major** [ˈmedʒɚ] 主修	I chose Business as my ma- jor in college. 我大學以商科作我的主修。
❺	**late** [let] 遲;晚	She never arrives on time; she is always late. 她從來不準時,她總是遲到。
❻	**interest** [ˈɪntərɪst] 興趣	I don't know what her inter- est is. 我不曉得她的興趣在那裡?

慣用語加強

❶ **to wait up** 熬夜等待

When his daughter goes on a date, he waits up for her.

當他女兒去約會,他就熬夜等她。

❷ **to have a good head for** 對某事有好頭腦

She has a good head for numbers.

她對數字有好頭腦。

❸ **to be interested in** 對某事感興趣

I am interested in teaching Chinese.

我對教中文很感興趣。

07 We may as well go home.

我們倒不如回家算了。

文法句型解析

❏ may as well做慣用語的說法，是「倒不如這麼做」或「還不如這麼做」的意思。也可以用might as well。

❏ 你們在看電視的球賽，但你們支持的隊伍卻大敗，越看越沒意思，你只好跟對方建議說，You may as well turn off the TV.

❏ 你們兩個人在家，對方問「今晚你想做什麼？」，你回答「不知道，你說呢？」，對方說「電視上有一部老電影要播放，還不錯。」，你覺得反正也沒其他事可做，就可以說，We might as well watch it.

標準會話一

A How's the team doing?
我們支持的隊，比賽進行得如何？

B Not so well.
不怎麼好哦。

We're losing by 50 points.
我們落後五十分。

A 50 points!
五十分啊！

You may as well turn off the TV.
你倒不如把電視關掉算了。

B You're right.
你說得沒錯。

There's only 5 minutes left in the game anyway.
反正比賽祇剩下五分鐘就結束了。

標準會話二

A Do you have any specials on pizza tonight?
你們今天晚上的比薩有沒有特價？

B Yes, it's "buy one, get one free".
有，今天是買一送一。

A Then you may as well give me a large.
那你就給我一個大的。

B What do you want on that?
你的披薩要加什麼料？

A Make them both with mushrooms, extra cheese, and pepperoni.
兩個都給我加蘑菇，多一點起司，還有義大利香腸。

標準會話三

A **Anything good on TV tonight?**
今晚電視上有什麼好節目嗎？

B No. Just a bad movie.
沒有，只是一部爛電影。

A **Might as well read a book, then.**
那還倒不如去看書呢。

B Yes.
是啊。

TV is a waste of time, anyway.
看電視本來就是在浪費時間。

增加字彙能力

	單字	例句
1	**anyway** [ˈɛnɪwe] 還是；反正	I don't need your help right now but thank you anyway. 我現在不需要你幫忙，但還是謝謝你。
2	**point** [pɔɪnt] 分數	He scored the most points of anyone on the team. 在整個隊裡面，他的分數算是最高的。
3	**pizza** [ˈpɪzə] 披薩餅	Pizza is a healthy fast food. 披薩是一種健康的速食。

❹	**special** [ˈspɛʃəl] 特價	A special is usually some-thing the store puts on sale. 特價就是指商店把東西拿來大拍賣。
❺	**TV** [ˈtiˈvi] 電視	TV is the abbreviation for "television". TV是television的縮寫。

慣用語加強

❶ buy one, get one free 買一送一

She loves sales that are "buy one, get one free."
她喜歡買一送一的拍賣。

❷ a waste of time 浪費時間

It's a waste of time to talk too much on the phone.
講太多電話是在浪費時間。

08　He may be smart, but he is lazy.

他也許聰明，但他很懶。

文法句型解析

❑ 我們前面學過may表示可能發生的事情，這裡要學的是加以應用，「事情可能是這樣，但還有其他的考慮因素在」，例如：你看到一雙很漂亮的鞋子，你的朋友提醒你，「可能真的是漂亮，但實用嗎？」，他會說They may be pretty, but are they practical?

標準會話一

A I love these new shoes!
我好喜歡這雙新鞋子。

B They may be pretty, but are they practical?
它們漂亮是漂亮，但它們實用嗎？

A Well, they're black and they will go with all my outfits.
噢，這雙鞋子是黑色的，跟我所有的服裝都可以配。

B Were they expensive?
它們很貴嗎？

A No, they were cheap.
不，它們很便宜。

B Then they sound like a good buy.
這樣聽起來，這雙鞋還蠻划算的。

標準會話二

A Did you hear about the seminar scheduled for next week?
你聽說過預計在下星期召開的講習會嗎？

B Yes.
聽說過。

I may try to go, but I don't know if I can fit it in.
我也許會試著參加，不過我不曉得我的時間是不是容納得下。

A This is a hectic time of year for you, isn't it?
現在剛好是一年裡面你很忙的時候，不是嗎？

B It sure is.
那確實是。

Are you going?
你要去參加嗎？

A I may go, but I had planned to take a personal day.
我也許會去，不過我已計劃好要請事假。

We'll see.
所以還要看看。

標準會話三

A I am excited to go to the Keng-Tin National Park next week.
下星期要去墾丁國家公園，我很興奮。

B How are you going to travel?
你要怎麼去呢？

A I may drive, but it takes so long.
我可能會開車，不過開車要好久。

B Have you considered taking the train?
你有沒有想過搭火車下去呢？

A That's a good idea!
那是一個好主意！

I'll call them for more information today.
我今天會打電話給他們問資訊。

增加字彙能力

❶	**hectic** [ˈhɛktɪk] 急；忙	She lived a hectic and busy lifestyle. 她的生活形態是又急又忙。
❷	**seminar** [ˈsɛmɪnɑr] 講習會	He attended the business seminar. 他參加了商務講習會。

❸	**practical** [ˈpræktɪkəl] 實用	She bought clothing that was practical. 她買服裝講究實用。
❹	**expensive** [ɪksˈpɛnsɪv] 貴的	The new gold watch was expensive. 這一個新的金錶很貴。
❺	**cheap** [tʃip] 便宜的	Dinner at the hamburger stand was cheap. 在賣漢堡的攤子上吃晚餐是很便宜的。
❻	**outfit** [ˈaʊtfɪt] 一套服裝	I need some outfits for parties. 我需要一些參加宴會的服裝。
❼	**excited** [ɪkˈsaɪtɪd] 興奮的	She was excited that she won first place. 她對贏得第一名，感到很興奮。

❶ fit in 硬排進

The doctor's office often had to fit in patients that didn't make an appointment.
醫生診所經常要硬排進一些沒有預約的病人

❷ good buy 很划算的買賣

The car has many features and a low price. It is a good buy.
這部車有很多附加的配件，價格又低，是一樁很划算的買賣。

09 Maybe it will stop raining soon.

也許雨很快就會停。

文法句型解析

❏ 前幾個單元裡說到「事情可能發生」,用 **may** 這個字。本單元要解說 **maybe** 的用法,表示「也許可以這麼做」,「也許是如此」或「也許會如此」。**maybe** 是個副詞,所以必須放在句首,「**Maybe+**某件事。」,例如:你說天氣可能會變好,Maybe the weather will get better.

❏ 上一句是指未來,但 **maybe** 也可以說「過去的事」,例如:某人要大門的鑰匙,你告訴他「也許瑪莉有」,說法是 Maybe Mary got it.,瑪莉若有鑰匙,早就有了,要用「過去式動詞」**got**。

標準會話一

A Can we go to the park?
我們可以到公園去嗎?

B No, it's too hot today.
不,今天太熱了。

A I really want to do something outside.
我實在想到戶外做做戶外活動。

B Maybe we can go swimming.
也許我們可以去游泳。

How does that sound?
你覺得如何呢？

標準會話二

A Do you have the access code to the new computer account?
你有沒有使用這個新電腦的戶頭密碼？

B No, but maybe Sue's got it.
沒有，蘇可能有。

A Does she still work in accounting department?
蘇還在會計部門工作嗎？

B No, she's upstairs in shipping and receiving department.
沒有，她現在在樓上的收發部門。

標準會話三

A Did you call about the concert?
你有沒有打電話去問那一場演唱會？

B There aren't any seats left for tonight's show.
今天晚上的表演，都已經沒有位子了。

A You mean it's sold out?
你的意思是說都客滿了？

B Yes, can you believe it?
是的，很難以置信吧？

A Well, maybe there are some seats for to-morrow night's performance.
那麼，也許明天晚上的表演還有一些位子吧。

B I doubt it.
我懷疑，不太可能。

It's a very hot ticket.
演唱會的票是非常熱門的。

增加字彙能力

①	**accounting** [ə'kauntɪŋ] 會計	The accounting department handles our bills. 會計部門處理我們的帳單。
②	**access code** ['æksɛsˌkod] 使用密碼	The access code keeps the information in the account private. 使用密碼保證戶頭裡的機密資訊。
③	**performance** [pə'fɔrməns] 表演	She gave a wonderful performance at the concert. 她在演唱會裡的表演太好了。

4	**concert** [ˈkɑnsɚt] 演唱會	I enjoyed the music at the concert. 我喜歡演唱會裡的音樂。
5	**outside** [ˈaʊtˈsaɪd] 戶外	My kids like to play outside. 我的小孩喜歡在戶外遊戲。
6	**doubt** [ˈdaʊt] 懷疑	The Chinese will win. No doubt about it. 中國隊一定贏，這點是毫無疑問的。

慣用語加強

❶ sold out 客滿；售罄

The movie tickets were all sold out.
電影票全部賣完了。

❷ have got；has got 有；得到

Mary has got a new car for her birthday.
瑪麗生日得到一部新車。

❸ hot ticket 熱門票

It was difficult to get into the show; it was a hot ticket.
想要進入這場表演非常困難，因為票很熱門。

第2篇　必需要理解

- 要求
- 義務
- 徵詢
- 意願的說法

10 Mary should get here soon.
瑪莉應該很快會抵達這裡。

文法句型解析

❏ should有很多意思和用法，不要急，我們一個單元只講解一個意思，並且有三個標準會話來舉例說明，跟著我的講解去讀，再配合會話的應用，你自能把should的所有用法徹底瞭解，自然純熟的應用，徹底增進你的英語會話能力。

❏ 本單元裡的should是表示「應該是會如此的」，例如：家人問你今天會晚一點回來嗎？你認為你應該會如往常一樣的時間到家(be home at the usual time)，你的回答就是：I should be home at the usual time.又如：瑪莉約好了此時要來，雖然她還沒到，但我們知道她不會遲到的，所以我們說Mary should get here soon.

標準會話一

A We've made good time so far on this trip.
我們這趟行程，時間還算很準。

B Yes, I think limiting our stops has helped.
是的，我想限制中途停車很有幫助。

A Do you think we'll make it by 9:30?
你想我們九點半以前到得了嗎？

B We should be there even earlier, like around 8:00 or so.
我們應該可以更早就抵達那裡，應該是八點左右吧！

標準會話二 在戲院門口

A How was the movie?
這部電影你看完覺得如何？

B Fun, real fun.
好玩，真的好玩。

You'd love it!
你會喜歡的。

Are you alone?
你自己一個人來看嗎？

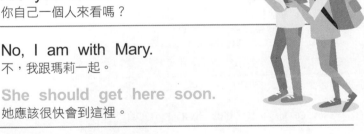

A No, I am with Mary.
不，我跟瑪莉一起。

She should get here soon.
她應該很快會到這裡。

B Well, enjoy the movie.
那，你們好好地看電影吧。

第 2 篇 必需要理解

A　Hi, Bob.
嗨！鮑伯

Come on in.
進來吧。

B　Thank you.
謝謝你。

Is Mary here?
瑪麗在這兒嗎？

A　No, but she should be back in just a minute.
不，不過她應該一會兒就回來的。

B　Do you mind if I wait?
我在這裡等，你介意嗎？

A　Not at all.
不會，不會。

Come into the living room.
進到客廳裡來吧！

增加字彙能力

	limit ['lɪmɪt] 限制	We limit ourselves to one glass of wine with dinner. 我們限制自己晚餐只喝一杯酒。
❶		

❷	**movie** [ˈmuvɪ] 電影	I can't wait to see the new movie. 我等不及要看這部新電影。
❸	**scary** [ˈskɛrɪ] 恐怖	Walking alone in the night is scary. 晚上自己一個人走路是很恐怖的。
❹	**earlier** [ˈɝlɪɚ] 較早	We went to bed earlier than usual. 我們比平常更早睡覺。
❺	**fun** [fʌn] 有趣	We had a fun time at the park. 我們在公園玩得很有趣。

慣用語加強

❶ just a minute 一會兒

Dinner will be ready in just a minute, so go wash your hands.

晚餐一會兒就好,所以去洗手吧!

❷ you would love 你會喜歡

You would love the new mall. Let's go tomorrow!

你會喜歡這個新購物中心,我們明天去吧!

11 I should write to her, but I was too busy.
我應該寫信給她,但我太忙了。

文法句型解析

❏ should也常用在表示「義務」、「給予建議」或「我們認為該件事很好,該去做」。例如:你知道你該讀書,也就是說讀書是你該做的「義務」,說法是I knew that I should study.

❏ 你的朋友知道你去看了一部電影,他問你電影好不好看,你覺得該部電影很好看,並鼓勵對方去看,也是要用should這個字,You should go and see it.你應該去看。

❏ 你的朋友喜歡抽煙,你卻認為抽煙對他的身體有害,要勸他戒煙(stop smoking),說法是You should stop smoking.

標準會話一

A Didn't I see you at the club last night?
我們昨晚不是在俱樂部看到你了嗎?

B Yes, I was there for a while.
是的,我在那裡待了一會兒。

A I thought you were going to hit the books last night?
我還以為你昨天晚上要讀書呢?

B Oh, I knew that I should study, but I needed to take a break.

哦，我知道我應該要讀書的，可是我需要休息一下。

標準會話二

A Your mom called.

令堂打電話來。

She sounded upset.

她聽起來不太高興。

She said she hadn't heard from you for some time.

她說她好久都沒有聽到你的消息了。

B I knew that I should write to her but I've been too busy.

我知道我應該給她寫信，但我實在是太忙了。

A She likes you to keep in touch, doesn't she?

她喜歡你跟她保持聯繫，不是嗎？

B I think she misses me.

我想她是在惦記我吧。

標準會話三

A How did the accident happen?

意外是怎麼發生的呢？

B I ran into another car.
我撞到了另一部車。

A I see you broke your arm.
我看得出你的手斷了。

B Yes.
是的。

I knew I should wear my seat belt, but I was just going around the block.
我知道我是應該要繫安全帶的，但我只是在附近繞一下而已啊。

I thought I didn't need to.
所以我認為我可以不用繫安全帶的。

A I'm glad you were not more seriously hurt.
我很高興你沒有受到更嚴重的傷害。

增加字彙能力

❶	**upset** [ˈʌpˈsɛt] 生氣	I was upset by the TV news. 我聽了這個電視新聞，感到很生氣。
❷	**accident** [ˈæksədn̩t] 意外事故	My car was wrecked in the accident. 我的車子在意外事故裡，全撞壞了。

3	**break** [brek] 名休息；弄斷	May I take a five-minute break? 我可以有五分鐘休息嗎？ Did you break your leg in the accident? 你在意外事件裡把你的腿弄斷了？
4	**block** [blɑk] 街段	We live one block from the store. 我們住的地方離那家商店一條街。
5	**seat belt** [ˈsit͵bɛlt] 汽車安全帶	Wear your seat belt every time you drive the car. 每當你開車時，都要繫好安全帶。
6	**seriously** [ˈsɪrɪəslɪ] 嚴重地	The workers were seriously hurt in the accident. 工人們在意外事故中受到重傷。

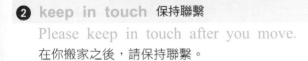

慣用語加強

1 **hear from** 接到音訊

I hope to hear from you soon.
我希望很快接到你的音訊。

2 **keep in touch** 保持聯繫

Please keep in touch after you move.
在你搬家之後，請保持聯繫。

3 **hit the books** 埋首苦讀

The test is tomorrow so I have to hit the books tonight.
明天要考試，所以我今天要埋首苦讀。

72 Should I ask for a raise?

我應該要求加薪嗎？

文法句型解析

❏ 在上一單元裡，我們學過should可以用來表示「提建議」，本單元是should這個用法的應用，用在「疑問句」，問對方的意見，例如：你正籌備一個宴會，你不知道該不該邀請瑪莉 (invite Mary to the party)，所以你問Should we invite Mary to the party?

❏ 你想要求加薪 (ask for a raise)，卻不知道是否可提出要求，所以你問Should I ask for a raise?

標準會話一

A Should I set an extra place at the table?
我應該在餐桌多安排一個位子嗎？

B Yes, I'm expecting Jane's boyfriend for dinner.
是的，我在等珍恩的男朋友來吃飯。

A Have you met him yet?
你見過他嗎？

B No, she's bringing him home for the first time tonight.
沒有，她今天晚上才第一次帶他到家裡來。

標準會話二

A Should I sign up for the Bible class on Wednesday night?
我應該註冊禮拜三晚上的聖經課程嗎？

B Who is teaching it?
是誰在教呢？

A Our minister from church.
是我們教會裡的牧師。

B Does he have a good reputation as a teacher?
他當老師的聲譽好不好呢？

A Yes, he's very well known in his field.
很好，他在他的領域裡是很出名的。

B Then by all means, sign up.
那麼你就一定要註冊。

標準會話三

A Should I order the steak or the fish?
我應該要點牛排還是魚排呢？

B Well, the fish comes with rice, and the steak comes with noodles.
哦，點魚排有飯，點牛排有麵。

A I'm trying to watch my weight.

我正試著控制我的體重。

B Then let's order the fish.

那麼就點魚排吧！

It's lo-cal.

它的卡路里熱量比較低。

增加字彙能力

❶	**boyfriend** [ˈbɔɪˌfrɛnd] 男朋友	Joe is Jane's boyfriend. 喬是珍恩的男朋友。
❷	**Bible** [ˈbaɪbḷ] 聖經	The Bible is a book about religion. 聖經是一本關於宗教的書。
❸	**minister** [ˈmɪnɪstɚ] 牧師	My minister teaches me about my life. 我的牧師在我的生活方面教導我。
❹	**reputation** [ˌrɛpjəˈteʃən] 聲譽	She had a bad reputation from drinking too much. 她喝酒喝太多了，聲譽不好。
❺	**lo-cal** [ˈloˌkæl] 低熱量	Lo-cal foods are good to eat when you are on a diet. 當你在節食的時候，吃低熱量的食物是很好的。

慣用語加強

❶ comes with 附送

Dinner comes with salad and dessert.

晚餐附送沙拉和甜點。

❷ to watch one's weight 注意體重

I'm watching my weight because I've gained too much.

因為我胖太多了,所以我正在注意體重。

❸ sign up 註冊

Have you signed up for the swimming lessons?

你有沒有註冊來學這個游泳課程呢?

❹ by all means 無論如何…

I will support you by all means.

無論如何,我會支持你的。

13 I should have phoned Mary, but I forgot.

我該打電話給瑪莉，但我忘了。

文法句型解析

❑ 注意：前面三個單元用的should是指現在或未來的事情。若說Mary should arrive at 9:00, but she didn't turn up.瑪莉應該在九點鐘抵達，但她沒出現。這句話是不對的，因為這裡說的是過去應該發生，而未發生的事。正確的說法是Mary should have arrived at 9:00, but she didn't turn up.

❑ 換句話說，當我們談到某件過去應該發生的事，卻沒發生，正確的句型是「某事+should have +過去分詞」，例如：你昨晚應該打電話給瑪莉(phone Mary)，你卻忘了打，說法是I should have phoned Mary.打電話的動詞是phone，在本句型裡要用過去分詞phoned。

標準會話一

A **There you are!**
你終於來了！

Why are you so late?
你為什麼這麼遲呢？

B **I should have called.**
我應該先打電話來的。

62

I'm sorry.
很對不起。

A I was worried about you.
我在為你擔心呢。

B I didn't know it would take so long to be here.
我不知道到這裡來，要花這麼長的時間。

A Next time, remember to call me.
下一次記得要先打電話給我。

標準會話二

A My stomach is upset.
我的胃不舒服。

B Did you eat breakfast this morning?
你今天早上吃早餐了嗎？

A Yes, but I should have had water instead of orange juice.
吃了，但我應該喝水而不要喝柳橙汁。

B Orange juice gives you a stomach-ache?
柳橙汁會讓你胃痛嗎？

A Yes.
是的。

It tastes great in the morning, but I pay for it later in the day.
早晨喝柳橙汁的滋味很美，但接著一整天我就要付出代價了。

標準會話三

A It's pouring outside.
外面正下著傾盆大雨。

B I should have brought my raincoat, but I was in too big a hurry!
我應該帶雨衣來的，但是我太匆忙了。

A That's okay.
那不要緊。

I can loan you mine.
我可以把我的借給你。

B You don't need it?
你不需要雨衣嗎？

A No.
不需要。

I brought my umbrella.
我帶了我的雨傘來。

增加字彙能力

①	**worried** [ˈwɝɪd] 擔心	I was worried about my new job. 我為了我的新工作擔心。

❷	**stomach-ache** [ˈstɑmək͵ek] 胃痛	When I am nervous, I get a stomach-ache. 當我緊張的時候，我就會胃痛。
❸	**orange juice** [͵ɔrɪndʒˈdʒjus] 柳橙汁	I like to drink orange juice. 我喜歡喝柳橙汁。
❹	**raincoat** [ˈren͵kot] 雨衣	She wore a yellow raincoat. 她穿了一件黃色的雨衣。
❺	**loan** [lon] 出借	I can loan you 5 dollars. 我可以借你五塊錢。
❻	**umbrella** [ʌmˈbrɛlə] 雨傘	You don't need an umbrella on a sunny day. 大晴天的，你不需要雨傘。

慣用語加強

❶ next time 下次

Next time you go to the store, remember to get more milk.

下次你到店裡的時候，記得要多買一些牛奶。

❷ to pay for it 付出代價

I didn't study. I'll pay for it tomorrow when I take the exam!

我沒讀書。明天當我考試時候，我可要付出代價。

❸ in a hurry 匆忙

I have got to go. I am in a hurry.

我必須走了，我急著有事。

14 Would you open the window?
請開窗好嗎？

文法句型解析

❑ 當你想請別人幫你做什麼事的時候，Would you先出口就對了，再來說你要請對方做的事，例如：想請對方開窗戶（open the window），只要先說Would you，那麼一句漂亮的英語Would you open the window? 就順口地說出了嘛！

❑ 因為是有求於人，盡量客氣總沒錯的，所以往往加個please。這個字有兩個地方可以放，說Would you please open the window?或是放在最後面，Would you open the window, please?都可以。

標準會話一

A Would you open the window, please?
請你把窗戶打開好嗎？

B Certainly.
當然啦。

It is warm in here.
這裡面熱得很。

A Yes.
是的。

I'm finding it hard to concentrate.
我發現很難專心的。

B Me, too.
我也是。

Is that open enough?
這樣開夠了嗎？

A That's fine.
這樣好。

The breeze will keep us awake.
微風可以讓我們清醒一點。

標準會話二

A Would you please pass the butter?
請你把牛奶遞過來好嗎？

B Here it is.
在這裡。

A Thank you.
謝謝你。

These rolls are delicious.
這些小麵包真好吃。

B Yes, my mother made them from scratch.
是的，那是我媽媽一手做的。

A I'm sorry this payment is late.
很抱歉這回付款遲了。

B We were just closing.
我們正要下班呢。

The manager's gone for the day.
經理已經下班了。

A Would you please put this in the manager's mailbox?
那請你把這個擺在經理的信箱好嗎？

B Of course.
當然可以。

There will be a late fee.
不過要交滯納金。

A Can I pay it next time?
我可以下次再付嗎？

B No, you must write a separate check and pay it now.
不行，你必須要另外再開一張支票，現在就付。

❶	**concentrate** [ˈkɑnsn̩ˌtret] 專心	It's hard to concentrate on your work when you are hungry. 當你肚子餓的時候，很難專注在你的工作上。
❷	**breeze** [briz] 和風	The cool breeze felt good on her warm face. 涼爽的和風吹在她熱熱的臉龐上，感覺很好。
❸	**manager** [ˈmænədʒɚ] 經理	He was the manager of the department. 他是這個部門的經理。
❹	**separate** [ˈsɛpəˌret] 分開的	We keep separate accounts at the bank. 我們在銀行裡的帳戶是分開的。
❺	**delicious** [dɪˈlɪʃəs] 好吃的	The fresh bread was delicious. 新鮮麵包真好吃。
❻	**mailbox** [ˈmelˌbɑks] 信箱	There are a lot of junk mail in my mailbox. 我的信箱裡面，有很多垃圾郵件。

❶ to find（事情）difficult 發覺某事很難

I find it difficult to believe you are only 15.
我發現非常難以相信你只有十五歲。

❷ from scratch 一手從零做起

She bakes all her cakes from scratch.
她所有的蛋糕，都是自己一手從頭製作烘烤的。

❸ gone for the day 下班了

It's near 6 o'clock. Everyone in the office is gone for the day.
已經快要六點，辦公室裡每一個人都下班了。

SCHOOL KID WORKPLACE

15 Would you like a cup of coffee?

你要喝杯咖啡嗎？

文法句型解析

❑ would like當做片語的用法，是表示「想要某件東西」或「想要做某件事」，表達的語氣很客氣。本單元要解說would like用在疑問句的用法。問Would you like+某件東西，表面上是問「你想要某件東西嗎？」，實際上是「提供某件東西」，是很客氣地在提議。例如：有客人到，你想倒杯飲料給他，你有好幾種飲料可以供對方選擇時，最好的說法就是Would you like anything to drink?你想喝點什麼嗎？

❑ 可是如果你只想倒杯咖啡(a cup of coffee)給對方，而不是供對方選擇時，說法就是Would you like a cup of coffee?你想喝杯咖啡嗎？

❑ 另一個用法是問「你要我幫你做什麼事嗎？」，其句型是「Would you like me to+原形動詞？」例如：你正要去買飲料，你想順便替對方買，你可以問他Would you like me to get you a drink?

❑ 你若是邀對方跟你去做某件事，而不是要給對方某件東西時，句型是「Would you like to+原形動詞？」，例如：你想邀對方去看電影(go to a movie)，應用本單元的句型就是，Would you like to go to a movie?

A Would you like a cup of coffee?
你要來杯咖啡嗎？

B No, thanks.
不，謝謝你。

I don't drink coffee in the morning.
我早上不喝咖啡的？

A Why not?
為什麼不喝呢？

A cup of good coffee would wake you up.
一杯好咖啡可以讓你清醒。

B I know.
我曉得。

But I like tea better.
但我比較喜歡茶。

A I am going to the soda machine.
我要去飲料販賣機。

Would you like me to get you a drink?
你要不要我幫你買飲料呢？

B No.
不要。

I am fine.
我還好。

A **Are you sure?**
真的嗎？

I don't mind.
我不介意幫你買哦。

B O.K., could you please get me a coke?
好吧，能不能請你幫我買一罐可樂？

A Absolutely!
沒問題！

I'll be right back.
我馬上就回來。

標準會話三

A Would you like to go bowling with us tomorrow evening?
你明天晚上要不要跟我們去打保齡球呢？

B It sounds like fun, but I can't go.
聽起來是很有趣，但我不能去。

I've got to study.
我必須要讀書。

A Oh, come on.
唉呀，別這樣。

It'll be fun.
打保齡球很好玩的。

B I really can't.
我真的不能去。

I've got an English exam on Monday that I'm really getting nervous about.
我禮拜一要考英文，我真的很緊張。

A O.K.
好吧！

Maybe next time.
也許等下一次吧！

Good luck on your exam.
祝你考試順利。

B Thanks.
謝謝你。

See you.
再見。

A Bye.
再見。

增加字彙能力

	wake [wek] 喚醒	Please wake me up at 6 o'clock tomorrow morning. 請明天早上六點把我喚醒。
1		

❷	**coffee** [ˈkɔfɪ] 咖啡	I drink strong, black coffee. 我喝濃而不加糖的咖啡。
❸	**soda** [ˈsodə] 汽水	I don't like soda. I drink water. 我不喜歡汽水，我只喝水。
❹	**machine** [məˈʃin] 機器	We bought a can-opening machine last night. 我昨天晚上買了一個開罐子的機器。
❺	**nervous** [ˈnɝvəs] 緊張	Please don't talk. You are making me nervous. 請不要說話，你讓我緊張。
❻	**exam** [ɪɡˈzæm] 考試	The final exam is coming. 期末考就要來了。

慣用語加強

❶ to get 人+物品 幫某人拿某物

I'll get you some paper.
我去幫你拿一些紙。

❷ good luck on 事情 祝某事順利

Good luck on your new job!
祝你新工作順利。

76 Would you prefer some tea?

你比較想喝點茶嗎？

文法句型解析

❏ 上一個單元「Would you like+某件東西？」的用法是，提供某件東西，沒得選了。本單元的用法加以變化，在Would you like的句後接上一句or would you prefer+另一件東西，給對方多一層選擇的機會。例如：上一單元提供咖啡Would you like a cup of coffee？你如果還有茶可供對方選擇，可以這樣說，Would you like a cup of coffee, or would you prefer tea?你要喝咖啡嗎，還是你較喜歡喝茶？

❏ 上一個單元，另一個用法「Would you like to +原形動詞？」表示「邀請對方去做某事」。同樣地，在本單元，你可以多加一樣讓對方選擇，「Would you like to+原形動詞，or would you prefer+動名詞？」注意：prefer這個字後面必須接動名詞。所以你若想讓對方選擇看電影或是看球賽都可以時，句子就是Would you like to go to a movie, or would you prefer going to a baseball game?

標準會話一

A **The dinner was wonderful.**
這頓晚餐真是太好了。

B **Now for dessert.**
現在是甜點的時間。

I have ice cream and cake.
我有冰淇淋和蛋糕。

A That sounds good.
聽起來都不錯。

B Would you like tea or would you prefer coffee with your dessert?
你吃甜點時,是想喝茶還是想喝點咖啡?

A Tea, please, with a little lemon.
請給我茶,加一點點檸檬。

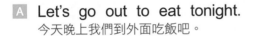

標準會話二

A Let's go out to eat tonight.
今天晚上我們到外面吃飯吧。

B Good idea.
好主意。

Would you like to go downtown or would you prefer going somewhere nearby?
你喜歡到市區裡吃,還是比較喜歡在這附近呢?

A Downtown sounds good.
市區裡聽起來不錯。

I want to try the new steak house.
我要試試新開的那一家牛排館。

B Me, too.
我也想試一下。

I heard it was wonderful.
我聽說那家館子很好的。

標準會話三 在商店裡，Ａ：顧客，Ｂ：店員

A I'd like to return these pants, please.
我想要退回這件褲子。

B Fine.
好的。

Is something wrong with them?
褲子有什麼問題嗎？

A They are the wrong color.
褲子的顏色不對。

B I see.
我明白了。

Would you like a cash refund, or would you prefer a store voucher?
你是想要現金退款或者你比較喜歡我們給你一張本店支票？

A I'd like a cash refund, please.
我想要現金退款。

B all right.
好吧。

I'll have it ready for you in a moment.
我馬上就給你準備好。

增加字彙能力

1	**ice cream** ['aɪs'krim] 冰淇淋	The ice cream was smooth and cool. 這個冰淇淋又順口又冰涼。
2	**prefer** [prɪ'fɝ] 較喜歡	I prefer drinking water. 我較喜歡喝水。
3	**downtown** ['daʊn'taʊn] 市中心	The office was in downtown. 辦公室在市中心。
4	**refund** [rɪ'fʌnd] 退費	I took the clothes back and got a refund. 我把衣服退了，並且得到退費。
5	**voucher** ['vaʊtʃɚ] 票據	The store gave me a voucher to spend on their products. 這家商店給我一張票據，可以用來買他們的商品。
6	**dessert** [dɪ'zɝt] 甜點	We had some dessert after dinner. 我們晚餐後，吃了一些甜點。

慣用語加強

1 sounds good 好主意

Dinner and a movie always sounds good to me after a hard day.

在一天努力工作之後，吃頓晚餐再看場電影，對我來講永遠是好主意。

2 in a moment 一會兒

I'll be back in a moment.

我一會兒就回來。

17 I would like to invite him over.
我想要邀他到家裡來。

文法句型解析

❏ would like to後面需接「原形動詞」，表示「我想要做某件事」。若是「想要邀請他過來(invite him over)」，就是I would like to invite him over.

❏ I would like to通常都說成I'd like to，想學道地美國腔調怎麼說，一定要聽CD。

標準會話一　在商店裡，A：顧客，B：店員

A This shirt is really nice.
這件襯衫真好。

I would like to try it on.
我想要試穿一下。

B Sure.
好的。

A Where are the changing rooms?
試穿室在什麼地方呢？

B Down this isle to the left.
沿著這個走道走下去，然後再左轉就是了。

標準會話二

A So what would you like to do after college?
那你大學畢業之後，想要做什麼呢？

B I'd like to pursue a career in advertising.
我想要追求廣告方面的事業。

A I assume your marketing degree will be useful in that area?
我猜想你的行銷學學位，在那一方面應該是很有用吧？

B I hope so.
但願如此。

I'll need some on-the-job training, too.
我還必須要有一些在職訓練。

A Do you know where you'd like to work?
你知道你喜歡在什麼公司上班嗎？

B Yes.
我知道。

I'd like to work for a nationally known magazine.
我想要在全國知名的雜誌社上班。

標準會話三

A I just got a phone call from management
主管剛剛給我打了一個電話。

B What did they say?
他們怎麼說？

A They offered me the new job!
他們要給我那個新職位！

B Congratulations!
恭喜你！

What did you say?
那你怎麼說呢？

A I said I'd like to think about it.
我說我想要再考慮考慮。

B You're kidding!
你不是開玩笑的吧！

What's to think about?
有什麼好考慮的呢？

A Well, it's a big change.
哦，算起來這是一個大變。

I need time to consider all my options.
我必須要時間考慮我所有的選擇。

增加字彙能力

1	**pursue** [pɚ'su] 追求	He went to graduate school to pursue his dream of getting his Ph.D. 他上研究所去追求他的博士夢。

❷	**congratulations** [kən͵grætʃəˈleʃənz] 恭喜	She offered her congratulations on his new position. 她對他的新職位表示恭賀之意。
❸	**consider** [kənˈsɪdɚ] 考慮	To consider is to think about something carefully. 考慮就是把某件事仔仔細細地想過。
❹	**changing room** [ˈtʃendʒɪŋ͵rum] 更衣室	A changing room is for people to try on new dresses. 更衣室是讓人們試穿新衣服的地方。
❺	**options** [ˈɑpʃənz] 選擇	I made a choice from a list of options. 我從一系列可能選擇的方案裡，做了一個選擇。

慣用語加強

❶ to try on 試穿

You should try on the shoes before you buy.
在你買這些鞋子之前，你應該試穿一下。

❷ on-the-job training 在職訓練

He didn't learn his job by going to school; he got on-the-job training from his employer.
他的工作技能不是在學校學到的，而是從雇主的在職訓練獲得的。

❸ You're kidding! 你是開玩笑的吧？

We say "You're kidding!" when we aren't sure if someone is telling the truth.
當我們不確知對方是不是在說真話的時候，我們說：「你是在開玩笑吧」。

MP3-19

18 Would you mind not smoking here?

可否請你別在這裡抽煙？

文法句型解析

❏ mind當動詞，表示「介意」的意思，Would you mind表面是問對方介不介意，卻是要求對方這麼做的意思。這是英語與中文不同之處，徹底瞭解之後，你的英語會話能力自能徹底增進。

❏ 注意：mind這個字後面一定要接「名詞」，所以若是「動詞」，要改成「動名詞」，也就是把動詞加ing。例如：你若想要求對方，在回家的路上順便把送去乾洗的衣物拿回來(pick up the dry cleaning)，你就可以這麼說Would you mind picking up the dry cleaning?

❏ 「Would you mind+你要對方做的事？」是要求對方去做某事。若是要求對方不要這麼做，英語的句型是「Would you mind not+你不要對方做的事？」，表面上是問「你是否會介意不這麼做？」，其實就是要求對方不要這麼做。例如：你要求對方別在這兒抽煙smoke here)，英語的道地說法就是Would you mind not smoking here?

標準會話一　　在餐廳裡，A：侍者，B：顧客

A Sir, would you mind not smoking here?
先生，可否請你別在這裡抽煙？

B Well, I asked to be seated in the "smoking" section.
怎麼，我是要求坐在抽煙區呀。

A I'm sorry.
很對不起。

That's across the room.
抽煙區在那一邊。

B Can you show me to a table there, please?
那請你帶我到那一邊的餐桌可以嗎？

A Certainly.
當然。

Right this way.
請從這裡走。

標準會話二

A Would you mind taking your child to the nursery?
可否請你把你的小孩帶到育嬰室？

B Is her crying bothering you?
她的哭聲干擾到你了嗎？

A Yes, it's hard to hear the speaker.
是的，我聽不清楚演講的人說的話。

B I'm sorry it's bothering you.
很對不起，她干擾到你。

A Don't get me wrong. I love kids.
不要錯怪我，我是喜歡小孩的。

I just really want to hear this talk.
只是我真的很想聽這場演講。

B No, I understand.
是的，我理解。

I would be happy to take her out of here.
我很樂意把她帶開。

標準會話三

A Would you mind picking up the dry cleaning today?
可否請你今天把送乾洗的衣物取回來？

B Okay.
好的。

How much is it?
那要多少錢呢？

A About 15 dollars.
大概十五元吧。

B I'll take a twenty from your wallet.
那我從你的錢包裡拿一張二十塊錢的。

增加字彙能力

1	**smoking** ['smokɪŋ] 抽煙	Smoking makes my eyes hurt. 別人抽煙讓我的眼睛好痛。
2	**bother** ['baðɚ] 騷擾；干擾	Am I bothering you by tapping my foot? 我的腳敲地板干擾到你了嗎？
3	**nursery** ['nɝsərɪ] 育嬰室	The children played in the nursery during the meeting. 會議的時候，小孩子在育嬰室裡玩。
4	**dry cleaning** ['draɪ,klinɪŋ] 乾洗	I'm going to pay for my dry cleaning. 我來付錢拿我乾洗的東西。
5	**wallet** ['wɑlɪt] 皮夾子；小錢包	I keep my money in my wallet. 我的錢都裝在皮夾子裡面。
6	**section** ['sɛkʃən] 區域	This section is for women only. 這一區是專給女士用的。
7	**understand** [,ʌndɚ'stænd] 明白	I understand what you are saying. 我明白你在說什麼。

第2篇　必需要理解

❶ don't get me wrong 別錯怪我

Don't get me wrong. I really like spaghetti, but I've had it four times this week.

別錯怪我,我真的喜歡義大利麵,不過我這個禮拜已經吃了四回了。

❷ right this way 從這裡走

Come right this way and I'll show you to your seat.

請從這裡走,我帶你到你的位置。

第3篇 英語會話

79 I must stop smoking.
我必須戒煙。

文法句型解析

❑ must有幾種用法,本單元所要教的用法是最基本、大家都熟悉的用法,是將must當作「必須」的意思。這個用法是表示説話的人認為「這件事有必要這麼做」。例如:我必須戒煙(stop smoking),表示你認為「戒煙是必須做的事」,所以用must,説 I must stop smoking.

標準會話一

A I must stop biting my nails!
我必須戒掉咬指甲的習慣。

B They do look unclean.
咬指甲看起來真的是不衛生。

A Do you know of a nail salon that will help me quit?
你知道這裡有修指甲的美容院,可以幫我戒掉這個習慣嗎?

B You don't need a salon.
你不用美容院的。

A I don't?
我不需要美容院?

B No.
不用。

Try painting some bitter liquid on your nails.
試著擦一些苦味的液體在你的指甲上。

Then you'll stop.
那你就可以戒掉了。

標準會話二

A I must turn my paper in by 5:00.
我必須在五點之前，把我的報告交上去。

B You'd better hurry.
那你最好趕快。

It's 4:30 now!
現在已經是四點半了！

A Can you give me a ride to the administration building?
你能開車送我到行政大樓嗎？

B Sure.
可以的。

Are you almost finished?
你快要寫完了嗎？

A Yes.
是的。

Just a few finishing touches and I'll be done.
只是幾個最後修正，我就做完了。

A I must stop eating so much junk food.
我必須要把吃那麼多垃圾食品的習慣戒掉。

B What do you eat?
你都吃些什麼東西？

A I eat potato chips, fries, and lots of candy.
我吃洋芋片、薯條，還有很多糖果。

B That is junk!
那真是垃圾！

Better stock up on some healthy snacks.
最好堆一些健康的零食吧！

增加字彙能力

❶	**nails** [nelz] 指甲	She had short, well-groomed nails. 她的指甲修得很齊。
❷	**salon** [sə'lɔn] 美容院	The salon fixed women's hair and did their nails, too. 這家美容院幫女士做髮型，也修她們的指甲。

3	**bitter** [ˈbɪtɚ] 苦的	Something is wrong. The water tastes bitter. 有點不對勁，這水嚐起來有苦味。
4	**liquid** [ˈlɪkwɪd] 液體	When ice melts, it becomes liquid. 當冰溶化時，它就變成液體。
5	**administration** [ˌædmɪnɪsˈtreʃən] 行政	The administration kept track of everyone enrolled in the college. 行政部門對大學裡，註冊有案的每一個學生都保有紀錄。
6	**junk food** [ˈdʒʌŋk͵fud] 垃圾食品；零食	Too much junk food is very bad for your health. 吃太多垃圾食品對你的健康是很不好的。
7	**healthy** [ˈhɛlθɪ] 健康的	She likes healthy foods like fruits and salads. 她喜歡健康的食品，比方説水果或沙拉。

慣用語加強

1 finishing touches 最後修正

He put the finishing touches on his project, then was ready to turn it in.

他在他的作品上，補了幾樣最後修正，然後就可以交了。

2 to stock up 儲備

She goes to the store once a month to stock up on supplies for school.

她一個月到店裡去一趟，好補充她的學校用品。

20 They must be tired.
他們一定累了。

文法句型解析

❏ must的第二種用法是根據種種情況判斷,「這件事肯定是這樣」,例如:你看到一部車子瘋狂地亂開,你說The driver must be crazy.司機必定是瘋了。這是根據車子開得很瘋狂的情況,你很肯定地這麼說。

❏ 因為你與瑪莉約好了,她要來你家,所以當你聽到門鈴聲時,你可以很肯定的說It must be Mary.門外按鈴的一定是瑪莉。

❏ 當對方告訴你,他今天中午沒吃午飯時,你當然也可以很肯定地說You must be hungry.你必定很餓了。

❏ 當你得知對方的兒子比賽得了第一名時,你自然可以流利地說You must be proud of him.你一定很以他為榮。,經過這些說明後,must表示「這件事肯定是這樣」這個用法很明確了,是嗎?今後,你不用再擔心must到底有幾種用法了。

標準會話一

A Did you see those cars?
你看了這些車輛沒有?

B They all ran the red light!
他們全都闖紅燈!

A That's very dangerous.
那真是危險。

How can they do that?
他們怎麼可以這麼做呢？

B Those drivers must be crazy.
那些司機一定都瘋了。

標準會話二

A I skipped lunch today.
我今天沒有吃午餐。

B You must be hungry.
那你一定餓了。

A I am!
我是很餓。

Please give me more rice.
請多給我一些飯。

B Okay, but save room for dessert!
好吧，不過要留一些胃口吃甜點哦！

A Don't worry.
別擔心。

I'll have room for dessert.
我會有胃口吃甜點的。

A Congratulations!
恭喜你！

Your son came in first in the race!
你兒子比賽得了第一名！

B That's great!
那太好了！

A You must be very proud of him.
你一定為他很感到驕傲吧。

B Yes, he practiced hard.
是啊，他練習得很賣力。

He deserved the first place.
他是應該得到第一名的。

增加字彙能力

①	**dangerous** [ˈdendʒərəs] 危險的	The shark is a dangerous fish. 鯊魚是一種危險的魚類。
②	**rice** [raɪs] 米飯	Most Chinese eat rice every day. 大部份的中國人每天都吃米飯。

③	**proud** [praʊd] 驕傲	I am proud of you. 我為你感到驕傲。
④	**practice** ['præktɪs] 練習	You must practice the piano every day. 你必須每天都練習彈鋼琴。
⑤	**race** [res] 比賽	Who do you think will win in the race? 你認為誰會贏得比賽呢？
⑥	**deserve** [dɪ'zɝv] 應得	He did something wrong and got punished. He deserved it. 他犯了錯受到懲罰，他是罪有應得。

慣用語加強

① to save room for 留點空位

Save room for the cake.
留點胃口好吃蛋糕吧。

② to skip （事物）跳過（事物）未做

I skipped the meeting and watched TV instead.
我沒有參加會議，跑去看電視了。

MP3-22

21

I must have left the key in the car.

我一定是把鑰匙留在車上了。

文法句型解析

❏ 上一個單元解說的是，你很肯定地說一個現在的情況。例如：對方出外旅行回來，你對他說 You must be tired. 你現在一定很累。

❏ 本單元要解說，你很肯定地在說過去的一個情況，用的是「**must have**+過去分詞」，例如：你前一天到瑪莉家，按了門鈴但沒人應門，所以，隔天你跟瑪莉說，You must have gone out. 你昨天一定是出去了。

❏ 瑪莉告訴你，昨天她打電話給你，但沒人接電話，但昨天你明明在家的，所以你肯定地知道，那時你一定是在睡覺(**be asleep**)，你就回答，I must have been asleep. 我一定是在睡覺。

❏ 你打電話要找瑪莉，但對方告訴你，沒有瑪莉這個人，你認為你一定是撥錯電話了(**dial the wrong number**)，因為撥電話這個動作，是發生在你講這句話之前，所以，你是很肯定地在說過去的一個情況，要說 I must have dialed the wrong number.

標準會話一

A I can't find my keys.
我找不到鑰匙。

B Did you look in your purse?
妳有沒有在錢包裡找一找？

A I looked in my purse and on the key rack.
我錢包裡和鑰匙串都找過了。

B Where could they be?
那他們會在什麼地方呢？

A Oh, I remember.
噢，我記起來了。
I must have left them in the car.
我一定把它們留在車裡了。

標準會話二　　打電話……☎

A Hello.
喂！喂！

Is Susan there?
蘇珊在家嗎？

B I'm sorry.
對不起。

There is no one by that name here.
這裡沒有人名叫蘇珊。

A I must have dialed the wrong number.
那我一定是撥錯號碼了。

B Were you trying to reach 555-6921?
你是想打555-6921號嗎？

A No, I was trying to reach another number.
不，我想打的是另一個號碼。

標準會話三

A I can't seem to get guestion 10 correct.
我老是沒有辦法把第十題做對。

B Did you check it with the answer?
你有沒有對照答案呢？

A Yes, I did.
有啊，我對照了。

I must have checked it 5 times.
我一定對照有五次之多了。

And it still isn't coming out right.
但答案仍然是不對的。

B Let me check your work.
讓我幫你檢查一下吧。

A Thanks for your help.
謝謝你的幫忙。

增加字彙能力

❶	**key** [ki] 鑰匙；答案	I put my keys on a key chain. 我把我的鑰匙擺在鑰匙鍊上。 Do you have the answer for the problems. 你有沒有這些問題的答案呢？
❷	**purse** [pɝs] 錢包	I carry my money in my purse. 我把錢放在錢包裡面。
❸	**reach** [ritʃ] 働找到	You can reach me at home during the day. 白天你可以在家找到我。
❹	**dial** [daɪl] 撥號	Dial the phone carefully. 打電話撥號的時候要小心。
❺	**correct** [kəˈrɛkt] 正確的	She finally got the correct answer. 她最後終於得到正確的答案。
❻	**remember** [rɪˈmɛmbɚ] 記得	I don't remember her name. 我記不得她的名字。
❼	**guestion** [ˈkwɛstʃən] 問題	Do you know the answer to the guestion? 你知道這個問題的解答嗎？

1 wrong number 號碼錯誤

She made a mistake in dialing and reached a wrong number.

她撥錯電話了，所以撥到另外一個號碼。

2 come out right 得到正確結果

She followed the recipe but the cake still did not come out right.

她一切遵照食譜，但烤出來的蛋糕還是不對。

22 We've got to go now.
我們現在必須走了。

文法句型解析

❏ have to 和have got to意思和用法是一樣的，在口語英語，
也就是美國人平常說話的時候，常用I've got to+原形動詞來
表示為了某種原因，必須這麼做。例如：你參加一個宴會，
很晚了你要離開，通常你會跟主人說，I've got to go now.

❏ 車子壞了，當然必須把它修好，車子通常都是送去修車場
請技工修理的，所以要用被動get it fixed。整句話就是，
We've got to get it fixed.

標準會話一

A This is a lovely party, but we've got to go now.
這個聚會真是溫馨。但我們現在必須走了。

B So soon?
那麼早啊？

A I'm afraid so.
恐怕是的。

My husband must get to work early tomorrow.
我先生明天早上一大早必須工作呢！

B I understand.
我理解。

Thank you for coming!
謝謝你們來參加。

A **Thank you for having us.**
謝謝你邀請我們過來。

標準會話二　　家庭裡，Ｗ：太太，Ｍ：先生

W **My car broke down again.**
我的車子又壞了。

M Again?
又壞了？

We've got to get it fixed.
我們得趕快把它修好。

W Can you take it on Monday?
你禮拜一可以把它送修嗎？

M I think so.
我想可以吧。

I'll get someone to run me home from work
if you can bring me in.
你要是可以載我去上班，我下班可以找人載我回家。

標準會話三 　家庭裡，W: 太太，M: 先生

M I've been too busy at work.
我工作實在一直都太忙了。

W Me, too.
我也是。

We've got to spend more time together.
我們必須要有更多時間在一起才行。

M Let's take Friday off.
那我們禮拜五都請假吧。

W We can go away for the weekend.
那我們這個周末就可到別的地方去。

M Yes.
是啊。

Let's plan on a nice weekend together.
我們計劃一下，這個周末好好聚一聚。

W Great!
太好了！

I can't wait.
我等不及了。

增加字彙能力

①	**lovely** [ˈlʌvlɪ] 可愛的	Her smile is always lovely. 她的微笑總是很可愛。

❷	early ['ɝlɪ] 早	She gets up early every day. 她每天早上都很早起床。
❸	busy ['bɪzɪ] 忙	I had a busy day at work. 我今天工作整天都很忙。
❹	party ['pɑrtɪ] 宴會	She invited several friends over for a party. 她邀了幾個朋友到家裡一起開宴會。
❺	together [tə'gɛðɚ] 一起	They enjoy doing things together. 他們喜歡一起做事情。
❻	weekend ['wik'ɛnd] 週末	Saturday and Sunday are the days of the weekend. 周末就是禮拜六和禮拜天。

慣用語加強

❶ take（某天）off 請假

I need to take one day off to see the doctor.
我必須請一天假去看醫生。

❷ I'm afraid so. 恐怕是如此

"Are you going to miss work on Friday?"
你禮拜五不打算上班嗎？

"I'm afraid so."
恐怕是如此。

❸ I can't wait. 我等不及了

I can't wait until vacation starts!
我等不及到放假開始。

23 If only I knew the code.
要是我知道密碼就好了！

文法句型解析

❏ 這個句型會讓你想到「假設法語氣」嗎？別去管這些文法名詞，本書要教你徹底增進英語會話能力，是採用自然英語學習法，把句型記住，遇到該用的情況，自然地使用，不要套文法，也不要逐字翻譯。

❏ 當你遇到某些情況，你真希望能有不同的情況時，該用的句型就是「If only+你所希望的情況」。記住，在「你所希望的情況」所用的句子，要用「過去式動詞」。例如：你因為不知道密碼而不能使用一個電腦程式，所以你一定很希望你知道該密碼(know the code)。知道該密碼(know the code)是你希望的情況，我們說過要注意，「你所希望的情況」要用「過去式動詞」，所以要用knew the code，整句話就是If only I knew the code.

標準會話一

A Are you still trying to access the program?
你還在試著要進入這個程式嗎？

B Yes, I am.
是的，我還在試。

If only I knew the code.
要是我知道密碼就好了。

第3篇 英語會話

A Did someone change it?
有人把密碼改了嗎？

B Yes, just yesterday.
是的，是昨天改的。

A Maybe you can call Bob.
也許你可以打電話給鮑伯。

He should know it.
他應該知道密碼。

B Good idea.
好主意。

It's too hard to figure out by myself.
想靠我自己把密碼猜出來實在太難了。

標準會話二

A Have you got your paper done?
你的學校報告做完了沒有。

B Not yet.
還沒有。

I still have four pages to type.
我還有四頁要打字。

A If only you had a computer!
要是你有一部電腦就好了。

You would be done in no time.
你可以立刻就做完。

B Well, you can bet that this is the last paper I type on a typewriter!
是啊，你可以打賭，這是我用打字機所打的最後一份報告了。

標準會話三

A This city is so interesting!
這個都市真是有意思。

If only we had more time to look around!
要是我們有更多時間可以四處看看就好了。

B There are too many landmarks to see in one day.
名勝太多了，一天看不完。

A Could we come back tomorrow?
我們可以明天再回來嗎？

B I don't see why not.
我想不出什麼理由不可以。

There are still several places I want to go.
還有幾個地方我也想去呢。

增加字彙能力

1	**code** [kod] 密碼	He memorized the code to his ATM card. 他把他的提款卡密碼背下來。

❷	**computer** [kəmˈpjutɚ] 電腦	Many people own computers now. 現在很多人擁有電腦了。
❸	**typewriter** [ˈtaɪpˌraɪtɚ] 打字機	Students used to use typewriters to write their papers. 從前學生是用打字機來打他們的報告。
❹	**landmarks** [ˈlændˌmɑrks] 名勝	There are many famous landmarks here in town. 本市這裏有很多著名的名勝。
❺	**yesterday** [ˈjɛstɚˌde] 昨天	We started school yesterday. 昨天學校開學。
❻	**bet** [bɛt] 打賭	I bet he doesn't know my name. 我打賭他不知道我的名字。

慣用語加強

❶ in no time 立刻

I can finish my work in no time when I am alone.
當我獨自一個人的時候，我可以立刻把我的工作做完。

❷ figure out 理解

Men are hard for women to figure out.
女人想理解男人是很困難的。

❸ look around 隨處看看

I told the salesman that I was just looking around.
我告訴店員說我只是隨處看看。

24 If only it would stop raining!
要是雨停了該有多好！

文法句型解析

❑ 又是一個「假設語氣」的用法，別擔心，我們會教你如何自然地應用，而不必去死背文法規則。

❑ 當你遇到一個情況，但你對這個情況並不滿意，你希望「會有不同的情況發生」，或是「希望別人能做某件事」。要表達這樣的期望，該用的句型是「**If only+主詞+would+原形動詞。**」

❑ 天正在下雨，瑪莉想出去，但不喜歡在雨中出去，所以她說，If only it would stop raining. 這就是我們說的，她不喜歡目前下雨的情況，她希望「雨會停」這個情況會發生。

❑ 約翰上班遲到，大家等著他，以至不能及早開會，所以大家就這麼說，If only John would come to work on time. 大家希望約翰能做到「準時來上班」這件事。

❑ 又如：隔壁把電視開得很大聲，吵到你了，你希望他們能「把電視關小聲一點」，說法就是 If only they would turn it down. 這兩個例子都是「你對現況不滿意，希望別人能做某件事」。

標準會話一

A I wish I could go with you, but I have to study.
但願我能跟你一起去，但是我必須讀書。

B If only you would do it tomorrow, we could go out together tonight.
要是你能明天再讀該有多好，我們今天晚上就可以出去了。

A No, it's best not to put it off until the last minute.
不，最好不要拖到最後一分鐘。

B You're right.
你說得對。

I'm glad you don't procrastinate.
我很高興你做事不因循怠惰。

標準會話二

A If only it would stop raining, we could go swimming.
要是雨停了有多好，我們就可以去游泳了。

B It's dangerous to swim during a thunderstorm.
在大雷雨裏去游泳是很危險的。

A Do you think it will clear up soon?
你認為天很快就會放晴嗎？

B Yes, I think so.
是的，我是這麼認為。

I see a break in the clouds over there.
我可以看出來那邊的雲有一些晴朗了。

標準會話三

A If only she would come to work on time, we could start these meetings sooner.

要是她上班準時該有多好，那我們就可以早一點召開這些會議。

B I don't know why she is always late.

我不知她為什麼總是遲到。

A Her car pool usually picks her up late.

和她共乘一部車的人通常比較晚去接她。

B Maybe she should drive by herself.

那也許她應該自己開車。

增加字彙能力

①	**procrastinate** [proˈkræstɪˌnet] 因循怠惰	He saves all his homework until the night before it is due. He loves to procrastinate. 他把他所有的功課留到要交的前一天晚上再做。他喜歡因循怠惰。
②	**tomorrow** [təˈmɑro] 明天	Tomorrow is the day following today. 今天過後的一天叫做明天。

❸	**dangerous** [ˈdendʒərəs] 危險	Going into the lion's cage is a dangerous idea. 鑽進獅子籠裏是個很危險的想法。
❹	**car pool** [ˈkɑrˌpul] 共乘一部車	They ride together to work in the same car pool. 他們共乘一部車一起去上班。
❺	**thunderstorm** [ˈθʌndəˈstɔrm] 大雷雨	There was a lot of lightening during the thunderstorm. 大雷雨的時候有許多閃電。

慣用語加強

❶ the last minute 最後一分鐘

He waited until the last minute to invite her to the dance.

他等到最後一分鐘才邀請她去參加舞會。

❷ clear up 天氣放晴

The sky cleared up quickly after the storm.

在暴風雨過後，天很快就放晴了。

❸ put off 拖延耽擱

Don't put off what you can do until tomorrow.

今日事，今日畢。

❹ pick（某人）up 開車接某人

Can you pick me up after work?

下班後你能不能開車來接我。

25 If only I hadn't slept over!

要是我不睡過頭就好了！

文法句型解析

❏ 這個句型是用在「懊悔過去所做的事不對，希望沒那麼做」，表達這個願望的用法是「If only+主詞+hadn't+過去分詞」，例如：對方昨晚在宴會上喝很多酒，以至於現在頭很痛，你真希望他昨晚沒有喝那麼多酒(drink so much wine)，注意這個句型的用法裡，動詞要用「過去分詞」所以要用drunk，整個句子就是If only you hadn't drunk so much wine last night.

標準會話一

A Are you all right?
你還好吧？

B My head aches terribly.
我的頭疼得厲害。

A If only you hadn't drunk so much wine at the party last night!
要是你昨晚在宴會裏不要喝那麼多酒就好了。

You would be feeling better now!
你現在應該就會覺得好一點。

第3篇 英語會話

B I know.
我知道。

It wasn't very smart, was it?
喝那麼多酒不太聰明的，不是嗎？

標準會話二

A If only I hadn't been so rude, I probably would have been invited to the professor's house.
要是我不要那麼魯莽無禮就好了，我也許就會獲得邀請到教授的家去了。

B How were you rude to her?
你對她又是怎樣的無禮法呢？

A I asked too many personal questions when I first met her.
我與她初次見面的時候，問她太多有關私人的問題。

B Well, nobody likes a busybody.
是嗎？沒有人喜歡愛管閒事的人。

標準會話三

A If only I hadn't voted for the tax increase!
要是我不投票贊成加稅就好了。

I wouldn't be seeing my paycheck go down the drain.
就不會眼睜睜看著我的薪水白白浪費掉。

B But we need the increased revenue to pay for the new schools.
可是我們需這些新增加的收入來蓋新學校啊。

A I guess the new schools are worth a few extra dollars.
我想新學校是值得我們多花一些錢吧。

B Yes, it's a good cause.
是的，那是一個好理由。

增加字彙能力

❶	**wine** [waɪn] 酒	He ordered red wine to go with his meal. 他點了紅酒佐餐。
❷	**rude** [rud] 無禮	The waiter was rude to us, so we left him a very small tip. 那個侍者對我們很無禮，所以我們給他很少的小費。
❸	**busybody** [ˈbɪzɪ͵bɑdɪ] 愛管閒事的人	She was a busybody, always prying into other people's business. 她是個愛管閒事的人，老是管到別人的事情上頭去。

④	**revenue** [ˈrɛvənju] 收入	The tax money provided extra revenue for the city. 這些稅錢為都市帶來了額外的收入。
⑤	**tax** [tæks] 稅	She paid the tax on her house. 她為房子付稅。
⑥	**cause** [kɔz] 理由	If we are going into a war, we'd better have a good cause. 如果要打仗的話，最好是有一個好理由。
⑦	**personal** [ˈpɝsṇəl] 私人的	Would you leave my personal stuff alone? 請你不要 我私人的東西！

慣用語加強

❶ personal questions 攸關私人的問題

Too many personal questions make people feel uncomfortable.

太多攸關私人的問題會讓人覺得不舒服。

❷ a good cause 充分的理由

The children's charity was a good cause.

支持兒童慈善事業是一個充分的理由。

❸ to go down the drain 白白浪費

A lot of money went down the drain in that project.

在那個工程計劃上有很多的錢白白浪費掉了。

26 Like his father, he's a born winner.
像他父親一樣，他是天生贏家。

文法句型解析

❏ 本單元和以下兩個單元在解說like和as這兩個字的用法，這兩個字都是「跟～一樣」的意思。但是，用法不一樣，like是個「介係詞」，後面需加「名詞」。而as是個「連接詞」，後面需接「句子」。

❏ 當我們要用英語表達「就像某人一樣」，或「就像某件東西一樣」時，「某人」或「某件東西」都是「名詞」，所以用介係詞，就是「Like+某人或某件東西」。例如：說約翰「就像他父親一樣」，就是Like his father，說完再繼續說哪一樣像他父親，例如：他很聰明(he is smart)。整句話就是，Like his father, he is smart.

標準會話一

Is your son captain of the baseball team and the debate team?
你兒子是棒球隊和辯論隊的隊長嗎？

Yes, he is.
是的。

Like his father, he's a born leader.
像他父親一樣他是個天生領導人。

You must be proud of him!
你一定非常以他為榮。

I am.
我是以他為榮。

But it's more important for him to feel proud of himself.
不過更重要的是，他要以自己為榮。

標準會話二

A I don't like this new mayor.
我不喜歡這位新市長。

B Why not?
為什麼不喜歡？

B Like a tree caught in the wind, he never knows which way to bend!
他就像一棵大樹在大風裏頭，不知道該往那個方向彎腰。

A You mean he's not very decisive?
你的意思是說他做事不果決。

B That's exactly what I mean.
那正是我的意思。

標準會話三

A That's a beautiful coat.
那是一件漂亮的外套。

Is it new?
那是新的嗎？

B Yes, I bought it at the boutique.
是的，我是在專賣店裏買的。

A Was it very expensive?
它很貴嗎？

B Well, like everything at the boutique, it wasn't cheap, but it was reasonable.
哦，就像是專賣店裏所有的東西一樣，它不便宜但還是合理的。

增加字彙能力

❶	**captain** [ˈkæptən] 隊長	She is captain of the team. 她是這個隊的隊長。
❷	**mayor** [ˈmeɚ] 市長	The mayor leads the city government. 市長領導市政府。

③	**decisive** [ˈdɪsaɪsɪv] 果決的	He is decisive, making decisions quickly. 他很果決，作決定很快。
④	**boutique** [buˈtik] 專賣店	The boutique sells women's clothing. 這個專賣店是賣女士的衣服。
⑤	**reasonable** [ˈriznəbḷ] 合理的	He paid a reasonable price for the car. 他付了合理的價錢買了這部車。

慣用語加強

❶ born leader 天生領導人

He's always been good at guiding others, being a born leader.

做為一個天生的領導人，他對引導別人非常在行。

❷ never knows 從不知道

She never knows what to do in a crisis.

她在危機裏從不知道該怎麼做。

27

As is well known, girls like to wear make-ups.

大家都知道，女生愛化妝。

文法句型解析

❏ 上一個單元我們說過，as是個「連接詞」，後面需接「一個句子」。本單元要解說的，是一個as的慣用語，「大家都知道」，它原本的說法應該是As that is well known，這裡的that is well known就是接在as後面的句子，可是，一般的說法，that都省略掉，變成As is well known.

標準會話一

A This exhibit is wonderful!
這一個展覽太好了！

B I'm very pleased with this museum.
我對這個博物館感到非常滿意。

A As is well known, it's famous for its collection of modern art.
大家都知道，這個博物館以收藏藝術品聞名。

B This is a lovely way to spend the afternoon in the museum.
參觀展覽真是打發下午時間的好方法。

標準會話二

A Do you have many women working in the city's administration office?
本市行政單位有很多女士工作嗎？

B Not at present.
現在還沒有很多。

But as is well known, we are working hard to hire more minorities.
不過大家都知道，我們正在努力要聘用更多少數族群。

A Do you have quotas to fill?
你們有聘用配額嗎？

B No.
沒有。

We prefer to choose our employees on the basis of their performance.
我們比較喜歡在工作表現的基礎上聘用我們的職員。

標準會話三

A Well, that famous trial is finally over.
你看，這一樁著名的審判終於結束了。

B Do you think the verdict was fair?
你認為判決是公平的嗎？

A No, not at all.
不，一點都不公平。

As is well known, the jury was rigged in favor of the defendant.
大家都知道，陪審團有偏見，偏向被告。

B I disagree.
我不同意你的看法。

I think our court system does a good job.
我認為我們的法庭制度表現得很好。

增加字彙能力

①	**exhibit** ['ɪgzɪbɪt] 展覽	The museum's exhibit of art was famous. 這個博物館藝術展覽很有名。
②	**verdict** ['vɝdɪkt] 判決	The jury returned a guilty verdict. 陪審團做出了有罪的判決。
③	**minority** [maɪ'nɔrətɪ] 少數民族	The black child was the only minority in his class. 這個黑人小孩是他們班上唯一的少數民族。

❹	**quota** [ˈkwotə] 配額	The quota was a fair way for all people to get a chance to work. 配額制是讓大家都能有機會工作的公平辦法。
❺	**rigged** [rɪgd] 被操縱的	The voting was not fair. It was rigged. 這個選舉不公平，被操縱了。
❻	**defendant** [dɪˈfɛndənt] 被告	He works for the defendant. 他為被告工作。

慣用語加強

❶ at present 目前

At present I am working on my college degree.
目前我正在攻讀大學學位。

❷ in favor of 偏向；贊同

He voted in favor of the new law.
他投票贊成這個新的法律。

MP3-29

28 I am sending you the bill, as was agreed.

照我們所同意，我把帳單寄給你。

文法句型解析

❏ 通常在講英語會話時，當我們做了某件事情，要告訴對方，很容易會就直接了當地說：我做了某某事。對方萬一記不起來曾經與你討論過那件事的做法，或是有意反悔，你就麻煩了，免不了要浪費口舌解釋，偏偏用英語解釋有時詞不達意，更是愈描愈黑。特別是外國人辦事，有時很斤斤計較，所以，你在說話的時候，補上一句「這是按照我們所同意的噢！」是最保險的說法。

❏ 當我們要說「照我們所同意的」，用as的用法，當然是「As it was agreed by us」，這裡的as是「正如」的意思，it是指某件事情，但口語的說法都把it和by us省略掉，變成As was agreed就可以了。

❏ agreed是agree去掉原本兩個e的最後一個，加上ed，在文法上稱agreed為agree的過去分詞，表示事情是「被雙方」所同意的。

標準會話一

A Are we ready for the planning meeting next week?
下星期的企劃會議我們都準備好了嗎？

B Yes.
是的。

I am sending you the agenda, as was agreed.
照我們所同意的，我正要把開會程序寄給你。

A Good.
太好了。

That way I can look it over and make any necessary changes.
那樣的話我就可以把程序看一下，做一些必要的更動。

B It should arrive tomorrow.
程序應該明天會到你那裏。

You have plenty of time.
你還有很多時間。

標準會話二

A I am looking forward to our lunch date tomorrow.
我期待著我們明天的午餐約會。

B Me, too.
我也是。

Are we still meeting at 2:00 P.M., as was agreed?
我們仍然照我們所同意的，下午兩點見面嗎？

A That's still a good time for me.
對我來講，那仍然是最恰當的時間。

B Then I will see you at the restaurant at 2:00 P.M.
那麼我們就下午兩點，在餐館見面了。

標準會話三

A My lawyer contacted me and said you are ready to settle the lawsuit.
我的律師跟我聯絡說你們對這項法庭訴訟準備和解。

B That's right.
一點都沒錯。

I am sending you the bill for my client's home repairs as was agreed.
按照我們所同意的，我會把我的委託人的房子修理帳單寄給你。

A Is that all?
只有那些帳單嗎？

B I will send you a bill for my attorney fees, also.
我也會把我的律師費用帳單寄給你。

A I'm relieved that we do not have to go to court over this matter.
我們不用為這件事上法庭，我感覺鬆了一口氣。

B Yes, I am satisfied. This is a good solution.
是的，我很滿意。這是個好的結果。

增加字彙能力

1	**agenda** [əˈdʒɛndə] 議程	The agenda lists all the subjects to be covered during the meeting. 會議議程列有會議當中，所有必須討論的所有主題。
2	**lawsuit** [ˈlɔ,sut] 訴訟	He brought a lawsuit against the business. 他對這家公司提起訴訟。
3	**attorney** [əˈtɝnɪ] 律師	Her attorney handled the legal matter. 她的律師處理所有法律問題。
4	**court** [kɔrt] 法庭	People settle legal problems in court. 人們在法庭解決所有法律問題。
5	**satisfied** [ˈsætɪsfaɪd] 滿意	He was satisfied that he had done a good job. 他對他自己表現良好感到滿意。
6	**matter** [ˈmætɚ] 事情	What's the matter with you? 你到底發生什麼事情？

	contact ['kɑntækt] 聯絡	I'll contact the school and set up a meeting.
7		我會跟學校聯絡，約定一個時間開會。

慣用語加強

1 **look over** 檢查一遍

Before I turned in my paper, I had looked it over.

在我把報告交出去之前，我檢查一遍。

2 **look forward to** 期盼

I look forward to seeing you soon.

我期待很快可以見到你。

第4篇 特殊用法

- 人
- 事
- 時
- 地
- 物……

29 Why don't you invite her?

你何不邀請她？

文法句型解析

❏ 大家都學過Why、What、How、When、Who這些疑問詞，也都知道它們的用法，在本書中不再重述。從本單元起到第四十二單元，要教你的是，把這些疑問詞自然應用到平常會話中。方法是教你基本的句型，你再把你要說的話帶入這個基本句型中，這個方法其實就是本公司每本書所強調的「自然英語學習法」。

❏ 每當你要向別人提個建議，希望他去做某件事時，可以用「Why don't you+建議他去做的事？」的句型，例如：你要建議對方「去邀請(invite)某人」，說法就是Why don't you invite her?或是你建議對方「把日期記在日曆上」(write the dates on a calendar)，應用本單元的基本句型，也就是Why don't you write the dates on the calendar?

標準會話一

A Have you met our new neighbors?
你見過我們的新鄰居了嗎？

B Not yet.
還沒有。

Why don't we invite them over for a cup of coffee and dessert?
我們何不邀請他們過來喝一杯咖啡吃些甜點。

A Good idea.
好主意。

Do you know their phone number?
你知道他們的電話號碼嗎？

B No, but Information may have it.
不，我不知道，不過詢問處可能會有。

標準會話二

A Why don't you write your mom instead of calling her?
你何不寫信給令堂而不要打電話給她。

B Calling is much more convenient.
打電話方便得多。

A Yes, but a letter is better.
是方便得多，但是書信比較好。

B Why do you think so?
你為什麼這麼認為？

A You can read a letter over and over.
你可以一遍又一遍地看信。

A call lasts just a few minutes.
而電話幾分鐘就過了。

A Did you remember that the Wang's are coming over for dinner tonight?
你還記得王家今天晚上要過來吃晚飯嗎？

B No, I didn't!
不，我不記得。

A Why don't you write these dates on a calendar?
你何不把這些日期記在日曆上呢？

B I should, but I can never find a minute to get organized.
我是應該這麼做的，但我總找不出時間來把這些東西弄得井井有條。

增加字彙能力

1	**neighbor** [ˈnebɚ] 鄰居	A neighbor lives close to you. 鄰居跟你住得很近。

❷	**Information** [ɪnfəˈmeʃən] 詢問處	Call Information to find out a phone number. 打電話給詢問處找電話號碼。
❸	**convenient** [kənˈvinjənt] 方便	I park in a convenient spot right next to my office door. 我把車子停在一個方便的位置，就在我辦公室門的旁邊。
❹	**better** [ˈbɛtɚ] 比較好	Cake is good, but I like candy better. 蛋糕是不錯，但我比較喜歡糖果。
❺	**organized** [ˈɔrgəˌnaɪzd] 井然有序	I need to get organized at home. 我必須把家裏弄得井然有序。

慣用語加強

❶ **come over** 邀人到家裡來

Are you coming over tonight?

你今晚要到我家來嗎？

❷ **find a minute** 找時間

When you find a minute, come talk to me.

當你有時間的時候，來跟我一談。

30 What if you are wrong?
要是你錯了,怎麼辦?

文法句型解析

❏ 當你想說「要是這種情況,怎麼辦?」時,只要記住「What if+某種情況?」這個句型,例如:你要說「要是我們錯了(we are wrong),怎麼辦?」,很簡單,就是用 What if we are wrong?

❏ 同樣地,想說「要是我們沒有準時做完(we don't finish it on time),怎麼辦?」,注意不要用中文去逐字翻譯,那會出現洋涇濱英語,外國人聽不懂的,只要套本單元的句型,就是 What if we don't finish it on time?

❏ 「What if+某種情況?」的句型,還可以用來表示「如果這麼做,你覺得好不好?」,例如:對方買了張新桌子,卻沒地方擺,你建議說「把舊桌子移到車房去(move the old one into the garage)」,這說法就是 What if we moved the old one into the garage?

❏ 注意在這個句子裡,把舊桌子移到車房去是一項建議,含有假設的語氣,句中的移 (move)要用「過去式」moved。

標準會話一 老師與學生,A:老師,B:學生

A The art project is due in two weeks.
這個勞作兩個禮拜要交。

138

B What if we don't finish it on time?
要是我們沒辦法準時做完怎麼辦？

A I do not accept late projects.
我不接受任何遲交的勞作作品。

B You mean we would get a zero?
你的意思是我們都得到零分囉？

A That's correct.
一點都沒錯。

B I guess we'd better make sure it's done on time, then!
那我想我們最好確定我們都能準時做完。

標準會話二

A I'm having a hard time figuring out where to put our new table.
我就是想不出來要把新桌子擺在什麼地方？

B What if we moved the old one into the garage and put the new one in the living room?
要是我們把舊桌子擺在車房，然後把新桌子擺在客廳，你看怎麼樣？

A Okay.
好吧。

Is there room in the garage?
車庫裏有位置嗎？

B It'll be a tight squeeze, but I think we can fit it in.
要擠得緊。不過我想我們可以把它擠進去的。

標準會話三

A Your first day of school is next Monday.
下星期一就是你開學的第一天。

B I'm kind of nervous about it.
我有一些緊張。

A What are you worried about?
你有什麼好擔心的呢？

B What if no one likes me?
要是沒有人喜歡我怎麼辦呢？

A Just give the kids a chance to get to know you.
你要給同學一個機會來認識你。

You'll be fine in no time.
然後你立刻就不會有問題了。

增加字彙能力

1	**zero** ['zɪro] 零分	If you get a zero in the exam, you'll fail the class. 你如果這次考試得零分，這一科你就會不及格了。
2	**garage** [gə'rɑʒ] 車庫	He parked the car in the garage. 他把他的車子停在車庫。
3	**school** [skul] 學校	They go to school every day. 他們每天都去上學。
4	**nervous** ['nɝvəs] 緊張	She gets nervous before exams. 她在考試之前感到很緊張。
5	**squeeze** ['skwiz] 擠壓	We squeezed oranges into juice. 我們把柳橙擠成汁。

慣用語加強

1 kind of 有些

She was kind of hungry, but didn't want dinner yet.

她有些餓，但還不想吃晚餐。

2 tight squeeze 擠得很緊

It was a tight squeeze, but she managed to fit into the dress.

雖然繃得很緊，但她還是想辦法把衣服穿上去了。

31 When it comes to math, I am the best.

談到數學，我最行！

文法句型解析

❏ When大家學過的是「什麼時候」的意思，這個用法我們不再贅述，本單元是教你when用在「When it comes to某件事，某人最行了。」的用法。

❏ 當你想說「談到某件事，某人最行了。」它的英語句型就是「When it comes to+某件事或做某件事～」。請注意：在這個句型，When it comes to的後面要接「名詞」，萬一說的是「做」某件事，本來是動詞，要改成動名詞，就是該動詞加ing。例如「談到電腦(computers)」，computers是名詞，那就沒問題。若是說談到「做頓好吃的飯」(make a good meal)，make是個「動詞」就需改成making：When it comes to making a good meal。

標準會話一

A I heard you are going camping with John this weekend.

我聽說你這個周末要跟約翰一起去露營。

B Yes, he told me to bring my fishing rod as there's a lake at the campground.

是的，他告訴我要帶釣魚竿，因為露營區有一個湖。

A When it comes to fishing, John is an expert.

談到釣魚，約翰是專家。

B I hope we really reel them in!

我希望我們真的把魚給釣上來。

標準會話二

A Did you get the bug out of your computer yet?

你把你的電腦錯誤糾正了沒有。

B Yes, Bob helped me find it.

糾正了，鮑伯幫我糾正錯誤的。

A When it comes to computers, Bob is the best.

談到電腦，鮑伯最行了。

B I know.

我知道。

I couldn't believe how fast he solved the problem for me.

我真難相信他那麼快就幫我把問題解決了。

第4篇 特殊用法

標準會話三

A Your mom is a great cook.
你媽媽是個好廚師。

B When it comes to making a good meal, she's the best!
談到做飯，她最行了。

A I wish my mom could cook like that.
我真希望我媽媽也能像那樣做那麼好吃的菜。

B Everyone has different talents.
每個人都有不同的天賦。

A That's true.
那倒是真的。

My mom sews really well.
我媽媽縫紉做得很好。

B Maybe they could teach each other some new tricks!
也許她們彼此可以互教幾招。

增加字彙能力

❶	**camping** [ˈkæmpɪŋ] 露營	I enjoy camping in the woods. 我喜歡在樹林裏露營。

❷	**fishing rod** [ˈfɪʃɪŋˌrɑd] 釣魚竿	He used the fishing rod to catch a big fish. 他用釣魚竿釣到一條大魚。
❸	**bug** [bʌg] 電腦程式錯誤	The computer program had a bug in it and was not working properly. 這個電腦程式有個錯誤，所以沒有辦法正常作業。
❹	**cook** [kʊk] 煮飯；廚師	Who cooks for you when your mom is not home? 令堂不在的時候誰幫你們做飯。
❺	**talent** [ˈtælənt] 天賦	She is a natural talent at dancing. 她對跳舞有天份。

慣用語加強

❶ **to reel in** 釣上鉤

The salesman had everyone's attention at the presentation, then he reeled them in with the sales pitch.

這個售貨員在簡報裏，把大家的注意力吸引過來，然後用銷售技巧把他們全部釣上鉤。

❷ **to teach new tricks** 教幾招新本事

The senior citizens taught the teenagers some new tricks on the dance floor.

這些老人教這些青少年幾招跳舞的本事。

第4篇 特殊用法

32 Who do you want to talk to?
你要找誰說話？

文法句型解析

❏ 在正式的英文文法中，當「誰」用作受詞時，要用whom，但是注意英語系國家人士講話時，大多用who而不用whom，這種語言的變化，非你我所能左右的。美國人怎麼說，我們就跟著怎麼說，絕不要自作聰明，講洋涇濱英語，要學道地的口語。所以問「你要跟誰說話？」，正確英語是Who do you want to talk to?

標準會話一

A This is the Public Library.
這是公共圖書館。

How may I help you?
可以為你服務嗎？

B I'd like to speak to someone in Reference, please.
我想要跟參考書部門的人說話。

A We have several people there.
那個部門有幾個人。

Who do you want to talk to?
你要找誰說話呢？

B It doesn't matter.
不要緊。

Anyone will do.
任何一個人都可以。

A Fine.
好吧。

I'll connect you to Reference.
我幫你接到參考書部。

標準會話二

A Who do you invite to your birthday party?
你邀請誰來參加你的生日宴會？

B Just some of the guys from the office, I guess.
大概是辦公室裏的幾個人吧，我想。

A What about your old school buddies?
那你的那些學校的老朋友呢？

B No, I've lost touch with most of them.
沒有，我與他們大部分都失去聯絡了。

標準會話三

A You can't cut in line!
你不能插隊。

Who do you think you are?
你自以為你是誰啊？

B Excuse me, but I was here first.
對不起，但是，是我先在這裏的。

A No, you weren't.
不，你不是。

I've been here the entire time.
我一直都在這裏的。

B You don't have to be so rude.
你也不用這麼無禮嘛。

A Wait your turn like the rest of us!
你必須像我們這裏所有人一樣，等著輪到你。

增加字彙能力

	public library 公共圖書館	He gets books out every week from the public library. 他每個星期向公共圖書館借書。
1		

❷	**reference** [ˈrɛfərəns] 參考書	The reference section has books like dictionaries and encyclopedias. 參考書部門有像字典或百科全書一類的書。
❸	**guys** [gaɪz] 男人	I play softball with the guys on Saturdays. 我每個星期六和男人打壘球。
❹	**buddy** [ˈbʌdɪ] 朋友	He was a good friend, my dear buddy. 他是個好朋友，是我親密的好朋友。
❺	**turn** [tɝn] 輪流	We each took a turn in the game. 我們每個人輪流玩遊戲。

慣用語加強

❶ to lose touch of 失去聯絡

I can't reach John. I might have lost touch with him.

我找不到約翰，我也許跟他失去聯絡了。

❷ wait your turn 等輪到你

Everyone will get a chance to play, so wait your turn patiently.

每個人都有機會玩，所以請耐心地等著輪到你。

33 Who cares?
管他的！

❏ 本單元要說明Who這個字用在口語「Who cares?」的用法。

❏ care是「在乎」的意思，Who cares?照字面翻譯，就是「誰會在乎？」，也就是「別去管它」，「沒有關係」的意思。

標準會話一

A I didn't get the part in the play that I tried out for.
我沒有獲得我去試演的那個角色。

B Who cares?
誰在乎？

It's just local theater, anyway.
那只不過是一個本地的小劇場而已。

A I care!
我在乎！

I tried hard and I'm disappointed.
我很努力的去嚐試了，我非常失望。

B There will be another show next month.
下個月還有一場表演。

You can try again.
你可以再試嘛。

A I'll give that some thought.
我會考慮一下。

標準會話二

A Did you study for the big test?
這個大考你讀書了沒有。

B No, but who cares?
不，但管它去的！

I'm going to fail it anyway.
我反正是不及格了。

A What a lousy attitude!
你這是什麼笨態度啊！

B I'm just being realistic.
我只是實際一點而已。

A No, you're just being lazy.
不，你只是懶惰而已。

A Did we get good seats for the game?
這一場比賽我們的座位好嗎？

B Who cares?
管它的！

I am just happy to be here.
能到這裏來我就很高興了。

A Well, I don't want to sit too far from the field.
是嗎？我不想坐在離球場太遠的地方。

B Don't worry.
不用擔心。

I'm sure we will be able to see the game no matter where we sit.
我確信不論我們坐在什麼地方，我們都能看到比賽。

增加字彙能力

❶	**play** [ple] ⑧話劇	We went to the theater to see a play. 我們到戲院去看一場戲劇。
❷	**fail** [fel] 失敗	Sometimes you must fail before you succeed. 有時你必須先失敗才能成功。

3	**lousy** [ˈlaʊzɪ] 很糟的	He had a headache and felt lousy. 他頭痛，情緒很不好。
4	**attitude** [ˈætɪtjud] 態度	His attitude was cheerful and positive. 他的態度是愉悦的、正面的。
5	**happy** [ˈhæpɪ] 快樂	I am smiling because I feel happy. 我笑是因為我覺得很快樂。

慣用語加強

❶ to give（某事）**some thought**
對某事多加考慮

I'll have to give that idea some thought before I agree to it.
在我同意這個想法之前我必須考慮考慮。

❷ no matter 不論

No matter where I go, I always meet friendly people.
不論我走到哪裏，我總是遇到友善的人。

34 Look who's talking!
你那有資格說我？

文法句型解析

❑ 這個句子好用得不得了，一定要會。但可別不懂亂用。別人講了，你也別按照字眼逐字翻譯成「看誰在說話？」，這樣翻譯笑話可就大了！

❑ 這是who在另一個口語中的說法，Look who's talking!其實就是中文成語裡的「五十步笑百步」。

❑ 當某人批評另一個人時，被批評的人認為對方也是一樣，沒有資格批評別人，就會頂回他一句Look who's talking!

標準會話一

A I can't believe you ate all the ice cream!
你把所有的冰淇淋都吃光了，我真難相信。

B Look who's talking!
你那有資格說我。

You ate all the chips!
你把所有的洋芋片吃光了。

A At least I went out and bought another bag.
最少我出去又買了一袋回來。

B Okay, I'll get more ice cream.
好吧，我就再買一些冰淇淋回來。

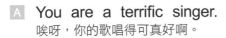

A You are a terrific singer.
唉呀，你的歌唱得可真好啊。

B Look who's talking!
你那有資格笑我。

You should sing in the choir!
你才應該去大合唱團裏唱歌呢。

A Maybe that's not such a bad idea.
也許那不是個壞主意。

Will you come, too?
你要不要跟我一起去唱啊？

B It would be fun to join a choir with you!
跟你這種人去唱合唱團那才有趣呢！

標準會話三

A You've been staying up late this past week.
這個星期你一直都在熬夜。

B Look who's talking!
五十步笑百步！

Did you make it to bed before midnight last night?
你昨晚到午夜之前還沒能上床睡覺呢！

A No.
是沒能上床睡覺。

I had some work to finish.
我有一些工作要做完。

B I think we both had better get to bed on time tonight.
我想今天晚上我們兩個都要準時睡覺。

增加字彙能力

1	**chips** [tʃɪps] 洋芋片	They enjoy chips with sandwiches for lunch. 他們午餐喜歡吃洋芋片和三明治。
2	**singer** [ˈsɪŋɚ] 歌手	The singer had a lovely voice. 這個歌手歌聲很甜美。
3	**choir** [kwaɪr] 合唱團	The choir sang many popular songs. 這個合唱團唱了很多著名的歌。
4	**join** [dʒɔɪn] 參加	Join us for dinner at our house. 來我們家跟我們一起吃晚飯吧。

⑤	**midnight** ['mɪdˌnaɪt] 午夜	He goes to bed around mid-night. 他大約在午夜上床睡覺。

慣用語加強

❶ at least 最少

At least he tries to get along with his co-workers; his partner doesn't try at all.

最少他還試著跟他的同事和平相處，他的同伴連試都不試。

❷ not such a bad idea 不是個壞主意

Going to bed early is not such a bad idea when you're tired.

當你疲倦的時候早點去睡覺不是個壞主意。

35 What would you say?
你意下如何？

文法句型解析

❏ 大家都學過what當「什麼」的用法，本單元我們來學What would you say?的用法。

❏ What would you say?照字面上的意思是「你會怎麼說？」，也就是問對方「你會有什麼意見？」。這句話用在對方還不知道某件事，你對他提這件事，並問他意見。用法是在這句話後面接if，再接「你要問對方意見的事」。例如：你已計畫好今年要提早去度假(go on vacation a little early this year)，你說「如果我告訴你(told you)我的計畫，你會有什麼意見？」，整個句子就是What would you say if I told you we are going on vacation a little early this year?句子似乎很長，但仔細聽CD，你會發現整句一氣呵成，不難！

標準會話一

A What would you say if I told you we are going on vacation a little early this year?
如果我告訴你今年我們要早點去度假，你會怎麼說？

B What do you mean?
你是什麼意思？

A I mean, I booked a cabin for May instead of July.
我是說，我訂了一間小木屋在五月，而不是在七月。

B Why?
為什麼呢？

A I found out the prices are a lot lower in May.
我發覺五月的價格低很多。

B Then I'd say, "Great!"
那我的意見就是「太好了！」

標準會話二

A What would you say if I asked you to come with me on the business trip?
如果我要求你跟我一起去出差，你意下如何呢？

B Why do you want me to accompany you?
你為什麼要我跟你一起去呢？

A I'll need your expertise with the new client.
對於這個新客戶，我需要你的專業知識。

B Since you put it that way, I'd love to go with you.
既然你這麼說的話，那麼我就跟你去吧。

標準會話三

A What would you say if I told you I could get the exam answers before the exam?
要是我跟你說我在考試之前就會拿到考試答案，你會怎麼說呢？

B Are you kidding?
你不是認真的吧？

A Not at all.
我不是在開玩笑。

I have a key to the professor's office.
我有鎖匙可以進到教授的辦公室。

B I'd say, "Don't try it or I'll report you!"
那我可要說「別嚐試，不然我可要去打你的小報告。」

A In that case, I guess I'd better lose the key.
那樣的話，我想我還不如把鎖匙丟掉算了。

增加字彙能力

	book [bʊk] 訂位	I booked a room in the hotel. 我在旅館訂了一間房間。
❶		

❷	**accompany** [əˈkʌmpənɪ] 陪伴	She wanted to accompany them on the trip. 她要陪伴他們去旅行。
❸	**client** [klaɪnt] 客戶	The client liked the work the company did for him. 這位客戶很喜歡這家公司為他所做的事。
❹	**expertise** [ˌɛkspɚˈtiz] 專業知識	I value your expertise. 我很珍惜你的專業知識。
❺	**report** [rɪˈport] 告狀	They had to report the lazy team member to the boss. 他們必須向老闆去告狀這個懶惰的組員。

慣用語加強

❶ since you put it that way 既然你這麼說

Since you put it that way, I guess I have to agree with you.
既然你這麼說的話，我想我必須要同意你。

❷ don't try it 不要嘗試

I will report any cheating I see, so don't try it.
只要我捉到作弊我一定去報告，所以不要嚐試。

36 What do you say?
你來說說你的意見吧！

文法句型解析

❏ What do you say?跟上一課的What would you say?一樣，都是在問對方的意見。

❏ 但是What would you say?是用在問對方「對某個計畫、某個提議，或某件事將會有什麼意見」，也就是說對方還不知道這件事，你正要告訴他。

❏ What do you day?是用在大家在談一件事，你問對方「你對這件事有什麼看法？」，也就是說，你問What do you say?時，對方已經知道你問的這件事。所以，在問What do you say?之前，事件已經被提出了。

標準會話一

A Bob, we're having a debate about the new property tax.
鮑伯，我們正在辯論新財產稅的事。

B I say it's too high.
我說財產稅太高了。

A And I say it's about time we had enough money to fix the roads.
我說現在應該是我們要收稅，讓我們有足夠的錢來修路的時候了。

B So, what do you say, Bob?
所以，鮑伯，你來說說你的意見吧。

A The salesclerk thought this was a good color on me.
售貨員認為這個顏色對我來說很合適。

What do you say?
你來說說你的意見吧？

B I think pink looks great on you.
我認為粉紅色在你身上看起來很好看。

A Is it too bright?
它會不會太明亮一些呢？

B No, you look just like a spring flower.
不會的，你看起來就像春天的花朵一樣。

標準會話三

A I'm thinking of buying a new car.
我在考慮要買一部新車。

B Have you tried that sporty model you've had your eye on?
你有沒有試試那一部，你一直在注意的跑車呢？

A Not yet.
還沒有。

The salesman said it wasn't right for me.
售車員說那部車不適合我。

B Who cares what he thinks!
你管他怎麼想呢！

What do you say?
你來說說你自己的意見吧。

A I've always wanted one of those.
我一直想要有一部那樣的車。

Maybe I'll go try one on for size.
也許我會去試試看合適不合適。

增加字彙能力

❶	**debate** [dɪˈbet] 辯論	The debate was over whether or not the law was fair. 不管法律是不是公平，這個辯論算是過去了。
❷	**property** [ˈprɑpɚtɪ] 財產	She owned some property in the country. 她在鄉下還有一些財產。
❸	**bright** [braɪt] 明亮	The bright color looked good on the pale woman. 皮膚白的女人穿明亮的衣服很好看。

❹	**sporty** [ˈspɔrtɪ] 跑車	The car was sporty and fun to drive. 這部車是一部跑車,開起來很有趣。
❺	**salesman** [ˈselzmən] 推銷員	People like the way that salesman doesn't pressure anyone to buy from him. 那個推銷員不給任何人壓力來向他買東西,這種方法人們很喜歡。

慣用語加強

❶ **it's about time** 是時候了

It's about time we started living within our budget.
是我們該量入為出的時候了。

❷ **try one on for size** 試試是否合適

Take a look at the new computers then try one on for size.
來看看這部電腦,然後試試是否合適。

37 What about me?
那我呢？

文法句型解析

❏ 「What about某人或某事」是另一個常用的英語，問「你覺得某人或某件事怎麼樣？」，例如：你要外出，擔心沒有人幫忙收信件，有人提出意見説「你認為我們的鄰居怎麼樣？可以託他們嗎？」，英語的説法就是，What about our neighbors?

標準會話一

A Did you get someone to take in our mail while we're gone?
當我們不在的時候，你有沒有找到人幫我們收郵件呢？

B I can't find anyone.
我找不到人。

A What about our neighbors upstairs?
那我們樓上的鄰居呢？

B Good thinking.
想得好。

I'd forgotten about them.
我差點把他們忘了。

A I don't know where to take my secretary for lunch.

我不知道要帶我的秘書去那裏吃午餐。

B What about that new deli on the corner?

街角的那間新美食店如何呢？

A Do you know if it's any good?

你知道它好不好嗎？

B I heard the food was so-so.

我聽說食物是差不多而已。

A I'm ready to call it a day.

我打算今天到此為止。

B I want to pack it in, too.

我也要開始打包回府了。

A Let's go out for a drink.

那我們去喝一杯酒吧。

B What about Mr. Wang?

那王先生呢？

Should we ask him to come along, too?

我們也要邀他一道去嗎？

A Sure.
當然了。

We've all had a long, hard day.
我們大家都做了好長、好辛苦的一天了。

增加字彙能力

1	**secretary** ['sɛkrə,tɛrɪ] 秘書	My secretary organized the office. 我的秘書把辦公室整理得井井有條。
2	**deli** ['dɛlɪ] 美食店	We got lunch meat for sand-wiches at the deli. 我們是在那家美食店買肉來做三明治。
3	**mail** [mel] 郵件	She sorted the company's mail. 她把公司的郵件分類。
4	**so-so** ['so'so] 馬馬虎虎	The movie wasn't terrible. It was so-so. 這部電影不是很難看,它還算馬馬虎虎。
5	**drink** [drɪŋk] 酒	He ordered a drink at the bar. 他在酒吧點了一杯酒。

慣用語加強

❶ call it a day 今天到此為止

I've done enough work; let's call it a day.

我做的工作足夠，我們今天到此為止吧。

❷ pack it in 打包回家

It's time to go home, so pack it in.

是回家的時候了，所以打包吧。

第4篇　特殊用法

38 When you get a minute, come see me.

你一有空就來見我。

文法句型解析

❏ 英語會話中，要叫別人幫你做事，可以用When you get a minute起頭，意思是「你一有時間時，就……」，後面的話隨便你提，任何帶點半命令的句子都可以。

❏ 當你有空的時候，When you get a minute，我有很多事，可以請你做，例如：come see me來看看我，stop by my desk到我辦公的地方來一下，give the front desk a call給服務台打個電話，walk the dog去遛一下狗，give me a hand來幫我一個忙。這麼好學常用的會話，現在就現學現用吧！

標準會話一

A When you get a minute, stop by my desk.
你有時間的時候，到我辦公的地方來一下。

B Is it about something pressing?
是很緊急的事情嗎？

A No, I just want to tell you about the upcoming conference.
不，我只是要告訴你馬上就要到來的會議。

B Great.
那好。

I'll be there after I finish entering these data.
我把這些資料輸入之後，我就到你那裏去。

標準會話二 在飯店

A When you get a minute, please give the front desk a call.
當你有時間時，打電話給服務台。

B Is there a message for me?
有人留話給我嗎？

A Yes.
有的。

When we got to the hotel room, the message light on the phone was blinking.
當我們到達旅館房間的時候，電話上的留言燈在閃爍著呢。

B It's probably my office.
那也許是從我辦公室來的留言。

I don't think it's urgent.
我想應該不是什麼緊急的事情。

A When you get a minute, let the dog out.
當你有空的時候,讓狗出去一下吧。

B Did you walk her today?
你今天帶狗去散步了嗎?

A Yes, but she still needs to go out.
出去了,不過牠還是想要出去。

B I'll put her on her rope and she can stay out all night.
那我就把牠綁在繩子上,牠可以整晚在外面。

A Okay.
好吧。

It's not going to be cold tonight.
今天晚上不會很冷的。

增加字彙能力

1	**data** ['dætə] 資料	She entered the data into the computer. 她把資料輸入電腦。
2	**front desk** 飯店服務台	She made her reservation at the front desk. 她在服務台預訂房間。

3	**pressing** [ˈprɛsɪŋ] 緊急	He hurried to his pressing appointment. 他匆匆趕赴緊急約會。
4	**blinking** [ˈblɪŋkɪŋ] 閃爍	The blinking yellow light means "caution." 交通號誌閃黃燈表示「小心」。
5	**urgent** [ˈɝdʒənt] 緊急	Something urgent needs attention right away. 有緊急的事情，現在需要馬上處理。

慣用語加強

1 **stop by** 短暫停留拜訪

Stop by and see us sometime.
找個時間到這裏來看我們吧。

2 **give a call** 打電話

Give me a call when you get home.
當你到家的時候打電話給我。

39 Where will I find you?
我要到哪裡找你呢？

文法句型解析

❏ Where是「哪裡」的意思，當你問「我該到哪裡找你？」，問的是未來的情形，所以應該要用Where will I find you？

標準會話一　在球場

A The crowds are incredible here!
真難相信這裏的觀眾這麼多。

B It is really hard to keep track of each other with so many people.
這麼多人，兩個人想不被擠散實在太難了。

A Hold my hand so we don't get separated.
握著我的手以免我們兩個被分開。

B If we do, where will I find you?
要是我們分開的話，我在哪裏可以找到你？

A Our seats are in section A23.
我們的座位在A23區。

B I'll meet you there if need be.
那如果需要的話，我就到那裏去找你好了。

A Are you coming to the airport to meet me?
你會到機場來見我嗎？

B Yes, I'm planning on picking you up.
會的，我打算開車去接你。

A Where will I find you?
那我在那裏可以找到你呢？

B Look for me near the airport security office.
在機場警衛室附近找我吧。

A Where is that?
機場警衛室在那裏？

B It's to the right of the taxi stand.
就在計程車排班處的右邊。

標準會話三　使用手機……

A I'm coming to your office to bring you the documents.
我正要來你的辦公室把文件交給你。

B Good.
好的。

Do you know where we are located?
你知道我們辦公室的位置嗎？

A You're on Second Street near the highway, right?
你們是在高速公路旁的第二街，對嗎？

B That's right.
對的。

Come to the 3rd floor.
請到三樓來。

A Where will I find you?
我要到那裏找你呢？

B My office is behind the black door.
我的辦公室就在黑門的後面。

1	**incredible** [ɪnˈkrɛdəbl̩] 難以置信	The colors of the beautiful sky were incredible. 美麗的天空五顏六色，真是難以相信。
2	**separate** [ˈsɛpəˌret] 分開	I separated the egg. 我把蛋分開。
3	**security** [sɪˈkjurətɪ] 安全警衛	Call security! Someone is trying to get in. 叫安全警衛！有人想要闖進來。

④	**document** [ˈdɑkjəmənt] 文件	She put the important documents in a safe place. 她把重要文件擺在安全的地方。
⑤	**located** [loˈketɪd] 位於	We are located on the corner of Chung-Cheng Road and Yung-Fu Street. 我們位於中正路和永福街的轉角。

慣用語加強

❶ to keep track of 注意位置所在

It's hard to keep track of small children.
我們很難注意小孩子的位置所在。

❷ if need be 如果必要的話

I can send the kids to my mother's, if need be.
如果必要的話,我可以把小孩送到我媽媽家。

40 How do you like your steak?

你想要幾分熟的牛排？

文法句型解析

❏ How是「如何」、「怎麼樣」的意思，本單元所要教你的是，how在英語會話中常見的幾個用法。

❏ How do you like your steak?表面上的翻譯是「你要你的牛排如何？」，你說牛排又能如何呢？實際上就是問「你想要幾分熟的牛排？」。這個句型可以應用到任何類似的情形，例如：How do you like your egg?(你的蛋要煮多熟？

❏ How do you like it?不是問「你如何喜歡它？」，而是問「你喜不喜歡它？」，這句話都是用在對方提到他有一個新的體驗，或新的東西；你都可以問How do you like it?你喜不喜歡？，例如：在談話中對方提到，他剛買了一部新的電腦，你可以問How do you like it?這句話中的it指的是那部電腦。

❏ How do you like+名詞，是上一種會話的應用。問How do you like it?時，彼此一定已知所談的是哪件事。若你要問對方喜不喜歡某件特定的事，就在How do you like後面接你要問的事，例如：你知道對方新買了一部電腦，你可以問，How do you like your new computer?你喜歡你的新電腦嗎？，又如：你知道對方現在剛開始自立更生的日子(live on one's own)，你可以問他How do you like living on your own?注意：這句話裡的live是動詞，要改成動名詞living。

標準會話一

A The grill is ready.
烤架已經準備好了。

How do you like your steak?
你要幾分熟的牛排呢？

B Rare, please.
三分熟。

A Do you want steak sauce on it?
你要加牛排醬嗎？

B No, thanks.
謝謝你，不用。

Just plain, please.
只要純牛排就好。

標準會話二

A How long have you lived here?
你在這裏住多久了？

B We've been here 6 months.
我們在這裏已經六個月了。

A How do you like it so far?
到目前為止你還喜歡嗎？

B The weather is fine and the people are very nice.
這裏天氣很好，人們也都很和善。

標準會話三

A How do you like living on your own?
自己賺錢養自己的生活你還喜歡嗎？

B It's harder than I thought.
比我想像的要困難。

A Why is that?
怎麼説呢？

B Oh, taking care of my home is difficult when I'm working to pay the bills.
哦，我要工作付帳單，又要照顧整個家，實在很困難。

A That's the price you pay for independence.
那是你為了獨立，所應該付出的付價。

增加字彙能力

1	**grill** [grɪl] 烤架	The grill has hot coals to cook the food. 烤架用熱炭來烤食物。
2	**rare** [rɛr] 半生不熟的	I like the meat red and rare. 我喜歡肉帶血，半生不熟。
3	**independence** [ˌɪndɪˈpɛndəns] 獨立	Independence is a good goal. 獨立是一個良好的目標。
4	**steak sauce** [ˈstek͵sɔs] 牛排醬	He spread steak sauce on his steak to make it taste better. 他把牛排醬抹在牛排上，讓它吃起來好吃一點。
5	**plain** [plen] 平凡	The dress was not decorated. It was plain. 這件衣服沒有裝飾，平凡得很。

慣用語加強

1 on one's own 自己養自己

He's been on his own since he was 18.
他從十八歲開始就自己養自己。

2 the price I pay 我得付出的代價

I hate being fat, but that's the price I pay for overeating.
我討厭肥胖，但是那是我吃太多的代價。

41 How's it going with your business?

你的生意可好？

文法句型解析

❏ How's it going?是英語最常用的打招呼語，比How are you? 更常見，下次你見到外國人時，不要再說How are you?了。 這可是你徹底增進英語會話實力的第一步，與美國人同步學 習英語。

❏ 如果你跟對方相熟，可以更精確地問他某件事最近做得如 何？只要加上with和另一個與主題有關的名詞就可以。

❏ 例如：對方是做生意的，你可以問How's it going with your business?你的生意可好？，又例如：你知道對方現在正在 忙著寫畢業論文，你就可以用How's it going with your dis- sertation?你的畢業論文寫得怎麼樣了？來打招呼。

標準會話一

A How's it going with your dissertation?
你的畢業論文寫得怎麼樣了？

B It's coming along.
還可以應付得上。

A When are you going to be finished?
你幾時可以寫完呢？

B By the spring, hopefully.
希望是到明年春天吧。

A Did you know I got a promotion?
你知道我獲得升遷了嗎？

B Yes, I did.
我知道。

How's it going with your new job?
你的新工作如何呢？

A I love it.
我很喜歡。

The work is interesting.
這份工作很有趣。

B I'm glad things are looking up for you.
我很高興你的事情越來越順利。

A How's it going with your mother-in-law's visit?
你岳母來拜訪，一切還好吧？

B So far, so good.
到目前還好。

A How long is she staying?
她要住多久呢？

B Long enough!
會住得夠久的！

增加字彙能力

1	**dissertation** [dɪsəˈteʃən] 畢業論文	He wrote his dissertation and received his Ph.D. 他寫了他的畢業論文並且拿到博士學位。
2	**mother-in-law** 岳母；婆婆	My wife's mother is my mother-in-law. 我太太的媽媽就是我的岳母。
3	**enough** [ɪˈnʌf] 足夠	I have enough money to go to the nice restaurant. 我有足夠的錢可以上那家好館子吃飯。
4	**hopefully** [ˈhopfəlɪ] 希望	Hopefully this dry weather will end soon. 希望這個乾旱的天氣很快就過去。

| ⑤ | **spring** [sprɪŋ]
春天 | Spring comes after winter.
春天是接著冬天而來。 |

慣用語加強

❶ things are looking up 事情越來越順利

I just got married and my job is great. Things are looking up.

我剛剛成家，而且我的工作越來越好，事情是越來越順利。

❷ coming along 一直在進行

My proposal is coming along and I will present it soon.

我的企畫案一直在進行，很快我就會針對它做一個簡報。

42 How about some music?

來點音樂如何？

文法句型解析

❏ 「How about+某件東西或某件事情？」是一種提議性的說法，在很多場合，你都會遇到需要向對方提供一些東西或提議做某件事，例如：朋友相聚，你提議要來一點音樂(some music)，很簡單，基本句型你已學過，把some music放進去就行了，How about some music?

❏ 你提議之事未必全是「名詞」如：music音樂，some wine 一些酒等，你可能提議要去看電影(go to a movie)，go to a movie是動詞，但是How about後面必須接名詞，很簡單，把go to a movie改成going to a movie，正確就是 How about going to a movie?去看一場電影好嗎？

標準會話一

A How about some music?
來一點音樂好嗎？

B Great.
很好。

Put on the CD that's in the stereo.
播放那片在立體音響裏面的雷射唱片吧。

A Is it classical?
它是古典音樂嗎？

B No, it's jazz.
不，那是爵士樂。

A How about some wine with dinner?
吃飯的時來點酒怎麼樣？

B No, thank you.
不，謝謝你。

A Do you mind if I have a glass?
那你介意我自己喝一杯嗎？

B Not at all.
不，不介意。

Go right ahead.
你儘管用吧。

A Have you thought of where we should take my parents tonight?
你有沒有想過，我們今天晚上應該帶我父母到那裏去玩呢？

B How about seeing the city gardens?
到市立公園去看看好嗎？

A Great idea.
好主意。

My mom is crazy about flowers.
我媽媽很喜歡花的。

B It will be lit up at night.
晚上那裏會燈光明媚。

增加字彙能力

1	**CD** 雷射唱片	All our favorite music is now on CD. 所有我喜歡的音樂現在都灌成雷射唱片了。
2	**classical** ['klæsɪkəl] 古典的	She listens to classical music. 她聽古典音樂。
3	**jazz** [dʒæz] 爵士樂	He plays the trumpet in a jazz band. 他在爵士樂團裏吹喇叭。
4	**gardens** ['gɑrdənz] 花園	I planted my gardens with many flowers. 我在我的花園裏栽了很多花。

| ⑤ | **glass** [glæs]
玻璃杯 | She filled the glass with water.
她在玻璃杯裏倒滿了水。 |

慣用語加強

❶ go right ahead 放手去做

Go right ahead and laugh, but I'm going to wear this hat!

你儘管笑吧,但我就是要戴這頂帽子。

❷ crazy about 很著迷

She's crazy about cats; she has 5 of them.

她對貓很著迷,她一共有五隻貓。

第5篇

最常用英語會話正則

43 I remember giving it to her.
我記得給了她。

文法句型解析

❑ 中學考英文最喜歡考的重點，remember到底要加動名詞還是不定詞的問題，説來好像是很頭疼的事，但英語會話中，卻是不能不會的句子。其實它是很容易弄清楚的，別緊張。

❑ 平常説「記得」某件事，百分之百用動名詞就沒錯。也就是説，在講話時，remember後面的動詞多説一個「英」的尾音，例如：把remember go説成remember go-ing，remember do説成remember do-ing，就對了。而going在文法上稱為go的動名詞，doing是do的動名詞。但説話時，你管它是什麼動名詞，只要多加一個ing(唸成英的尾音就可以了。

❑ 整句話用「I remember+動名詞」這個説法，表示「我記得我做了這件事」，例如，你記得你把電腦關了turn off the computer)，説法就是I remember turning off the computer.

標準會話一

Ⓐ Miss Lin says she can't find the file you wanted.
林小姐説她找不到你要的檔案。

B I remember giving it to her.
我記得我是給了她的。

A Are you positive she has it?
你非常肯定她有那個檔案嗎？

B Positive.
我非常肯定。

Tell her to look in the large filing cabinet.
告訴她在那個大檔案櫃裏找一找。

標準會話二

A The doctor's office charged us for that missed appointment.
我們預約掛號沒有去，但那個醫生的診所還是跟我們算錢。

B But I remember calling to cancel it!
但我記得我打電話給他們取消了啊！

A Well, here's the bill.
是嗎？這裏是帳單。

B I'll have to get to the bottom of this.
我叫要好好的追究一下這件事。

I'm sure I canceled it.
我確定我已經取消了。

標準會話三

A I love showing you where I grew up!
我很樂意帶你看看我成長的地方。

B What's this park up ahead?
前面這個公園是什麼公園？

A I remember playing here when I was a little girl.
我記得我還是個小女孩的時候都在這裏玩。

B Does it still look the same to you?
這裏看起來還是一樣的嗎？

A In a way, yes, although I have certainly changed since then.
在某方面可以這麼說。不過我自己從那時候到現在卻已經是變了。

增加字彙能力

①	**positive** [ˈpɑzətɪv] 肯定	I am positive I returned the library book. 我很肯定我已經把圖書館的書還了。
②	**charged** [ˈtʃɑrdʒd] 收費	The mechanic charged us too much to get our car fixed. 這個技工修理我們的車收費太高了。

3	**missed** [mɪst] 錯過	I missed my train and had to take a taxi. 我錯過火車，所以必須搭計乘車。
4	**park** [pɑrk] 公園	The park had lots of trees. 公園有很多樹。
5	**show** [ʃo] 展示某人	I enjoy showing you the places I love to go. 我很樂意把我喜歡去的地方展示給你看。

慣用語加強

1 **to get to the bottom of** 追究清楚

I finally got to the bottom of that financial problem and discovered what had gone wrong.

我終於把那個財務問題追究清楚，並且發現哪裏出錯了。

2 **up ahead** 前面

The sign said "dangerous curves up ahead."

那個牌子説「前面有危險彎路」。

44 Do you think we should leave?
你認為我們該走了嗎?

文法句型解析

❏ 本單元是教你「徵詢別人的看法」怎麼說。

❏ 它的基本句型是「**Do you think**+你要徵詢別人看法的事?」例如:你想知道對方到明天能把報告做完嗎(finish the report by tomorrow)?使用本單元教你的句型,你自可以流利的說Do you think you could finish the report by tomorrow?

❏ 有沒有注意到,上一句的think是現在式,而could卻是過去式?其實could與時間沒有關係,它是表示「可能」的意思,所以用could。

標準會話一

A Do you think you could finish the report by tomorrow?
你認為到明天之前可以把這篇報告完成嗎?

B Why?
怎麼了?

Is there a deadline?
這個報告有截止日期嗎?

A Sort of.
大概可以這麼說吧。

I'm going out of town this weekend.
這個周末我要外出不在這裏。

B All right.
那好吧。

That's good enough for me.
依我看這篇報告已經夠好了。

I'll have it done by tomorrow morning.
我明天早上之前就把它弄好。

標準會話二

A Do you think we should walk to school or take the bus?
你認為我們應該走路上學或者是搭公車呢？

B We have time to walk if you want to.
我們還有時間可以用走的，如果你想走路的話。

A It's good exercise.
走路是個好的運 。

B We both could use a little more of that.
我們兩個應該好好運 一下。

A Let's get going.
那就走吧。

A Do you think this dish has enough salt in it?
你認為這道菜鹽下得夠嗎？

B I don't know, but it does taste like something is missing.
我不曉得，不過它嚐起來總覺得好像少了點什麼東西。

A I followed the recipe to the letter.
我是一字不漏照著食譜做的。

B Sometimes you have to use your intuition when you are cooking.
有時候你做菜要用一下自己的直覺。

增加字彙能力

1	**deadline** [ˈdɛdˌlaɪn] 截止日期	She has to get her work done by the deadline. 她必須在截止日期之前把工作做完。
2	**bus** [bʌs] 公共汽車	The bus was crowded on the way to work. 在上班途中公車很擁擠。
3	**exercise** [ˈɛksɚˌsaɪz] 運動	I exercise to keep my body healthy. 我運動以保持體魄健康。

④	**salt** [sɔlt] 鹽	Add salt only after you taste your food. 你要先嚐過你的食物之後才加鹽。
⑤	**intuition** [ˌɪntuˈɪʃən] 直覺	Her intuition tells her when things are not quite right, even when they seem fine. 當事情有些不對的時候，她的直覺會感覺出來，即使那些事情表面看起來沒什麼不對。

慣用語加強

❶ good enough 夠好了

I don't need a fancy house; my apartment is good enough.

我不需要美侖美奐的房子，我的公寓就已經夠好了。

❷ to the letter 逐字逐句

They followed the rules to the letter.

他們遵從規定已經到了逐字逐句的地步。

❸ something is missing 少點什麼

I feel like something is missing.

我覺得少了一點什麼。

45 I'm sure you're right.
我確定你是對的。

文法句型解析

❏ 有些話你直接説出來，會給人很無力的感覺，前面多加一句，有時可以把你的意思表達得更好，例如：有人提議要去逛百貨公司，你知道這麼早，百貨公司還沒開門，你若只説It's closed this early in the morning.你所説的話就顯得可有可無，加個「我很確定」I'm sure，就變成I'm sure it's closed this early in the morning.是不是搶眼多了。

❏ 在一句話之前加上I'm sure不僅有加強説話份量的作用，有時還可用在勸慰對方，向對方保證事情應該不是那樣的，例如：對方告訴你，某人對她説了一些髒話，你可以説I'm sure he didn't mean them.我確定他不是那個意思。這裡使用I'm sure是用來勸慰對方。

標準會話一

A He said some ugly things to me.
他對我説了一些不堪入耳的事。

B I'm sure he didn't mean them.
我確定他沒有那種意思。

A Oh yes he did!
哦，他就是那種意思。

B No, people say things they don't mean when they are mad.
不，當人們生氣的時候，他們會說一些他們不是有意要說的話。

A Do you really think so?
你真的是這樣想的嗎？

B Yes, I do.
是，我真的是這樣想。

Don't give it another thought.
你不要多心了。

標準會話二

A Let's go to the mall.
我們到購物中心去吧。

B I'm sure it's closed this early in the morning.
早上這麼早，我確定他們還沒開始營業。

A What time does it open?
那它們幾點開門呢？

B Probably after 10 o'clock.
大概要到十點以後。

A The boss just fired me!
我老闆把我炒魷魚了！

B I'm sure he didn't mean to.
我很確信他不會有意把你炒魷魚的。

A What makes you say that?
你怎麼會這麼說？

B You're an excellent worker.
你是個很傑出的員工。

Besides, he always talks before he thinks on Monday morning!
更何況，星期一早上，他講話是不經過大腦的。

增加字彙能力

❶	**ugly** [ˈʌglɪ] 醜陋的	His ugly words made her feel bad. 他所使用的醜陋字眼使她覺得很難過。
❷	**mad** [mæd] 生氣	I stayed out of his way when he was mad. 當他生氣的時候我就不去惹他。

❸	**closed** [klozd] 打烊；關著	The door was closed. 門是關著的。
❹	**fired** [faɪrd] 開除；炒魷魚	He got fired by the company for always coming in late. 他因為經常遲到被公司開革了。
❺	**excellent** [ˈɛksələnt] 傑出	She was an excellent wife. 她是個很好的太太。

慣用語加強

❶ don't give it another thought 不用多心

When someone is mean to you, don't give it another thought. He is having a bad day.

當有人對你兇的時候，不用多心，他只不過是那天事事不順罷了。

❷ to talk before you think 不經大腦說話

It can be embarrassing to talk before you think.

說話不經大腦，有時候會弄得很不好意思。

46 Am I allowed to date?

我可以約會嗎?

文法句型解析

❑ 有時候你會遇到,在某個場合你不知道某件事可不可以做,你要知道答案,英語有兩種問法:「Am I allowed to+你想做的事?」或「Is it OK to+你想做的事?」例如:你想把車子停在某個地方,但是不知道那個地方你可不可以停,問一聲Am I allowed to park here?就知道了。又如:你在某個博物館裡,你不知道在那裡可不可以照相 (take pictures),還是同一個句型Am I allowed to take pictures?

標準會話一

A Am I allowed to write this off on my taxes?

我在報稅的時候,可以把這些報銷嗎?

B You have to be careful about that sort of thing.

你對報稅這種事一定要小心一點。

A The laws are so complicated!

法律太複雜了。

B That's why you hired an accountant.

那就是為什麼你請我當你的會計師。

標準會話二

A Am I allowed to park here?
我可以把車子停在這裏嗎？

B No, that space is clearly marked for handi-capped people.
不行，這個位置很明顯標示是要給殘障朋友的。

A I'm sorry.
對不起。

I didn't see the sign.
我沒有看到這個牌子。

B Make sure you pay close attention.
你要小心，好好注意一下。

You could be fined for parking there.
在這裏停車可能就會被罰款了。

標準會話三

A Am I allowed to have meat on this diet?
這一套飲食計劃中，我可以吃肉嗎？

B No, only chicken or fish.
不行，只能吃雞或是魚。

A Why no meat?
為什麼不能吃肉呢？

B We're trying to lower your cholesterol, and meat has too much fat.

我們試著要減低你的膽固醇，而肉有太多油脂。

增加字彙能力

1	**complicated** ['kɑmplɪˌketɪd] 複雜的	He didn't understand the complicated directions. 他不了解這份複雜的說明。
2	**handicapped** ['hændɪˌkæpt] 殘障的	The handicapped woman uses a wheel chair. 這個殘障婦女使用輪椅。
3	**fine** [faɪn] ⑩罰款	The police officer fined the man for speeding in his car. 這個人開車超速，被警員罰款。
4	**diet** ['daɪət] 飲食	His diet was healthy. 他的飲食很健康。
5	**cholesterol** [kə'lɛstəˌrol] 膽固醇	He was careful not to have too much cholesterol because he wanted to keep his heart healthy. 他很小心不要有太多膽固醇，因為他要保持心臟的健康。

❶ to write off 攤銷

He asked if he could write off his travel expenses.
他問說他是不是可以把出差費用攤銷掉。

❷ clearly marked 明顯標示

The police car was clearly marked so that people knew it was an official car.
警車標示得非常清楚，以便人們可以知道那是一部警車。

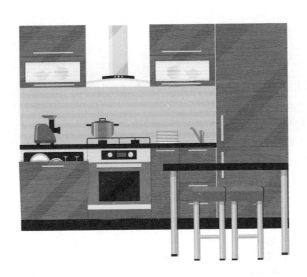

47 Is it OK to cash the check here?

在此兌現支票可以嗎？

文法句型解析

❑ 本單元的句型跟上一單元的用法一樣，只是換一個句型，
例如：上一單元裡問Am I allowed to park here?，用本
單元的句型就是Is it OK to park here?

標準會話一

A Is it OK to leave my car behind the building?

把我的車留在這棟大樓後面可以嗎？

B No, we have a special parking lot across the street.

不行，我們在街對面有特留的停車場。

A Do I need a sticker for my windshield?

我需要拿一張停車貼紙貼在我的擋風玻璃上嗎？

B Yes, you'll get one as soon as we can print one up.

是的，我們把貼紙印出來就給你。

標準會話二

A Is it OK for me to go now?
我現在可以走了嗎?

B Yes, we're done for the day.
是的,今天的事都做完了。

A I'm going to be late tomorrow.
我明天會遲一點到。

B That's understandable.
那是可以理解的。

We put in a lot of hours this week.
我們這個星期工作時間非常長。

標準會話三

A Is it OK to turn in this project next week?
下星期才交這份作品可以嗎?

B Are you having some trouble with it?
你遇到困難是不是?

A Not really.
不完全是。

I wanted to take a trip with a friend and need a little extra time.
我要跟朋友出去玩,所以我需要額外的時間。

B Get your priorities straight.
你可要把重要順序弄清。

Forget the trip and do your work.
不要去旅行，做工作吧。

增加字彙能力

❶	**parking lot** 停車場	The parking lot was full, so he parked on the street. 停車場客滿，所以他把車子停在街邊。
❷	**sticker** ['stɪkɚ] 貼紙	Make sure you show the sticker to the parking man, or he won't let you leave your car in the company's lot. 你注意要把貼紙展示給停車管理員，不然他不會讓你把車子停在公司的停車場。
❸	**windshield** ['wɪndˌʃild] 擋風玻璃	A rock cracked the car's windshield. 一顆石頭打破了這部車子的擋風玻璃。
❹	**friend**　[frɛnd] 朋友	My husband is my dearest friend. 我的先生是我最親蜜的朋友。

| ❺ | priorities
[praɪˈɑrətɪz]
優先順序 | He has his priorities in the right order.
他的優先順序排得非常正確。 |

慣用語加強

❶ put in a lot of hours 工作很長時間

They put in a lot of hours on the project then took the next week off.

他們在那個專案上，工作了很長的時間，然後在隔週休息。

❷ to get one's priorities straight
把（某人的）優先順序弄清楚

If you think play comes before work, you need to get your priorities straight.

如果你認為玩比工作重要，那你可要好好把優先順序弄清楚。

48 As far as I am concerned.
就我個人來說。

文法句型解析

❏ as far as I am concerned是一句英語會話中常用的片語，用在有人詢問你的意見時。表示「就我個人來說」或「依我的看法是」，放在你的意見之前或之後都可以，例如：As far as I'm concerned, you're okay.在我看來，你應該沒有問題。或The present mayor is doing fine as far as I'm concerned.就我個人來看，現任市長做得不錯。

標準會話一

A Should we go to lunch at the Mexican or the Chinese restaurant?
我們應該去墨西哥或者中國餐館吃午餐呢？

B As far as I am concerned, I don't care one way or another.
對我個人來說，去那個餐館我都不在乎。

A Which one is closer?
那一種館子比較近？

B The Mexican restaurant is closer to the office.
墨西哥館子離公司比較近。

A Then let's go there so we can get back on time.

那我們就上墨西哥館子吧，這樣我們可以準時回來。

標準會話二

A Do you think it will rain again today?

你認為今天還會下雨嗎？

B As far as I'm concerned, it can rain all it wants to.

就我個人來說，它愛下雨儘管去下。

A Why do you say that?

你怎麼這麼說呢？

B Because my grass needs all the water it can get.

因為我的草需要越多水越好。

標準會話三

A Do you know who you want to vote for in the coming election?

在這即將到來的選舉當中，你決定選誰嗎？

B As far as I'm concerned, the person we have now is doing fine.

就我來說，我們現任的這位就做得不錯。

A So you don't want to elect anyone new?
那麼你是不打算選任何新的人了？

B I don't think so.
我想不會。

The other candidates don't have as much experience.
其他的候選人沒有那麼多經驗。

增加字彙能力

❶	**Mexican** ['mɛksɪkən] 墨西哥人；墨西哥的	The Mexican food was spicy and delicious. 墨西哥食物很辣卻很好吃。
❷	**Chinese** [tʃaɪ'niz] 中國人；中國的	The Chinese painting was done with delicate colors. 中國國畫用色很細膩。
❸	**candidates** ['kændɪˌdets] 候選人	None of the candidates was truly qualified. 這些候選人裏面沒有一個真正有資格。
❹	**elect** [ɪ'lɛkt] 選舉	In the US, we elect a new president every 4 years. 在美國，我們每隔四年選一次新總統。

	experience [ɪks'pɪrɪəns] 經驗	She has 12 years of office experience. 她有十二年的辦公經驗。
5		

慣用語加強

1 one way or another 無論是什麼方法

Even if he doesn't have time, he's going on the vacation one way or another.

縱使他沒有時間,他還是會想辦法去度假。

2 all（it）wants to 盡其可能的

That dog can bark all it wants to; I'm not getting up to let it out.

那條狗可以盡可能的叫,我是不會放牠出去的。

49 I see you have a comment on this.

我看得出，對此你有話要說。

文法句型解析

❏ I see後面接著一個句子，表示「我看得出」、「我知道這件事」、「我看到某件事」。

❏ I see若表示「我看得出」時，後面的句子可以用「現在式」或「過去式」。例如：I see you are upset. What's wrong?我看得出你不高興。怎麼一回事？或者是I see you had something to say in the meeting. Why didn't you speak out?我看得出剛剛在會議時你有話要說。為什麼不說出來呢？

❏ I see若表示「我知道這件事」或「我看到某件事」，後面的句子一定要用「過去式」，因為你知道或看到的事情已經發生了，如：I see you made the Top Ten List for this month.我看見你這個月上了十大的榜單。或I see you got an A in your math class. 我知道你的數學得了「A」。

標準會話一

A I see you made the Top Ten List for this month.

我看見你這個月上了十大的榜單。

B Yes, I sold the highest number of houses in our real estate office.
是的，在我們的不動產公司裏，我這個月賣的房子最多。

A You did a great job!
你的表現太好了！

B It was hard work, but I'm thrilled to be doing so well.
我的工作很賣力，不過我還是很驚訝我做得這麼好。

標準會話二

A I see you wrote a suggestion for the suggestion box.
我看到你寫了一個建議投到建議箱裏。

B Yes.
是的。

I hope the management sees it.
我希望經理會看得見。

A What did you say?
你建議什麼呢？

B I suggested the management give us our bonuses in private instead of in a big ceremony.
我建議經理把紅利私下給我們，不要大肆慶祝。

A I see you got an A in your marketing class.
我知道你的行銷學得了一個Ａ。

B I'm glad you noticed!
我很高興你注意到了！

A I may seem hard on you at times, but I notice your good grades as well as those that aren't so good.
有時候我似乎對你比較嚴格，但是我注意到你的好成績，也注意到那些個不怎麼好的。

B I know, Dad.
爸爸，我曉得。

You just want me to do well.
你的目的只是要我表現得好一些。

增加字彙能力

①	**real estate** 不動產	She sold real estate as her career. 她以賣不動產做為她的事業。
②	**thrilled**　['θrɪld] 訝異	I was thrilled to get a raise. 我很訝異獲得加薪。

	bonus ['bonəs] 紅利；獎金	We get a Christmas bonus every year. 我們每年都得到聖誕節獎金。
3		
4	private ['praɪvɪt] 私下；不公開	He is a shy, private person. 他是一個害羞不公開的人。
5	grades [gredz] 成績	The teacher gave grades to the class. 老師向全班發成績單。

慣用語加強

1 Top Ten 十大（傑出榜）

He was one of the Top Ten in sales this year.
他是今年銷售部門十大傑出榜的一員。

2 suggestion box 意見箱

The suggestion box contains good ideas for company improvement.
意見箱裏有改善公司的好意見。

50 Please tell me how you make it.

請告訴我你是怎麼做的。

 文法句型解析

❑ 這個單元的基本句型就是在教你，如何請對方告訴你某件事該怎麼做，或某件事對方是怎麼做到的。

❑ 「請告訴我」，英語很簡單：Pease tell me.在本單元裡的用法是後面接how you，再接「你想知道怎麼做的事」，例如：你想知道，對方如何做蛋糕(make the cake)，英語說法就是Please tell me how you make the cake.。要問「如何跑這個電腦程式」run this program，就是用Please tell me how you run this program.請告訴我，你是怎麼樣跑這個電腦程式。

❑ 注意，問對方「某件事你是如何做到的」，how you manage that，這句話中的manage這個字，就是「成功地把某件事做到」的意思。

標準會話一

A This pie is delicious.
這個派真好吃。

Please tell me how you make it.
請告訴我你是怎麼做的。

B It's easy.
那簡單。

You need a can of cherries and a pie crust from the store.
你需要一罐櫻桃罐頭和一張從店裏買的派皮。

A That's it?
只要這樣就行了嗎？

B It's just that simple!
就是這麼簡單。

標準會話二

A You always seem so happy.
你看起來總是這麼快樂。

Please tell me how you manage that.
請告訴你是怎麼做到的。

B I have a lot of faith, and I know everything works out eventually.
我有很深的宗教信仰，而且我相信凡事最終總會解決的。

A Do you really believe that?
你真的相信嗎？

B Oh yes!
哦！真的相信！

Ever since I was little, my faith has seen me through.
從我很小的時候開始，我的宗教信心就一直在引導著我。

A Please tell me how you run this program.
請告訴我你怎麼樣跑這個電腦程式。

I'm really at a loss to figure it out.
我真的糊塗了，想不出所以然來。

B You have the disk in the wrong drive.
你把磁碟片擺到錯誤的磁碟機上面去了。

A Are you sure?
真的嗎？

B Trust me. I've been using this program for over a year.
相信我，我用這套程式已經超過一年了。

A Then I guess you know what you're doing!
那我猜想你知道你在幹嘛吧！

增加字彙能力

	pie crust 派皮；餅皮	The pie crust was brown and flaky. 這個派的皮已成金黃色，而且一層一層的很脆。
❶		

2	**cherries** [ˈtʃɛrɪz] 櫻桃	She put red cherries on the dessert. 她把紅櫻桃擺到甜點上去。
3	**faith** [feθ] 信心	Her faith is important to her. 她的信心對她很重要。
4	**eventually** [ɪˈvɛntʃʊəlɪ] 最終	Eventually I'd like to retire to the beach. 最終我要退休，搬到海邊去享受。
5	**disk** [dɪsk] 磁碟	He put the information on the disk and mailed it to her. 他把資訊寫到磁碟片上去並且寄給她。

慣用語加強

❶ to see through 引導度過

Her patience saw her through many difficult times.
她的耐心引導她度過很多困難的日子。

❷ at a loss 迷糊了

I'm at a loss to explain the situation.
我自己都糊塗了解釋不出這個情形。

好流利！ 我的第一本英語會話與文法

英語系列：53

．．．

作者／施孝昌
出版者／哈福企業有限公司
地址／新北市板橋區五權街16號
電話／(02) 2808-6545　傳真／(02) 2808-6545
郵政劃撥／31598840　戶名／哈福企業有限公司
出版日期／2019年2月
定價／NT$ 299元 (附MP3)

．．．

全球華文國際市場總代理／采舍國際有限公司
地址／新北市中和區中山路2段366巷10號3樓
電話／(02) 8245-8786　傳真／(02) 8245-8718
網址／www.silkbook.com　新絲路華文網

．．．

香港澳門總經銷／和平圖書有限公司
地址／香港柴灣嘉業街12號百樂門大廈17樓
電話／(852) 2804-6687　傳真／(852) 2804-6409
定價／港幣100元 (附MP3)

．．．

email／haanet68@Gmail.com
網址／Haa-net.com
facebook／Haa-net 哈福網路商城

．．．

圖片／shutterstock
Copyright © 2019 HAFU Co., Ltd.
著作權所有　翻印必究
如有破損或裝訂缺頁，請寄回本公司更換

Origenal copyright © Talk a lot in English

國家圖書館出版品預行編目資料

好流利！ 我的第一本英語會話與文法 /
施孝昌著. -- 新北市：哈福企業, 2019.2
　　面；　公分. -- (英語系列；53)

ISBN 978-986-96282-9-7(平裝附光碟片)

1.英語 2.讀本

805.165　　　　　　　　108000036